To ...

with all best wishes from

Neil

September 2010

BURNING DESIRE

BURNING DESIRE
AND OTHER SHORT STORIES

NEIL BUTTER

Burning Desire and Other Short Stories

Copyright © 2010 by Neil Butter

All rights reserved. No part of this publication may be reproduced, stored in a retrieval system, or transmitted in any form or by means, electronic, mechanical, photocopying, recording, or otherwise, without the prior permission of the publisher.

This is a work of fiction and, as such, it is a product of the author's creative imagination. All names of characters appearing in these pages are fictitious except for those of public figures. Any similarities of characters to real persons, whether living or dead, excepting public figures, is coincidental. Any resemblance of incidents portrayed in this book to actual events, other than public events, is likewise coincidental.

ISBN 978-1-4457-2155-2

By the same author:

Doctor George and Other Short Stories.

Contents

PREFACE	vii
BURNING DESIRE **or THE SALAMANDER SYNDROME**	1
PEARLY GATES	5
THE WEDDING TOAST	9
DILEMMAS	13
METHOD IN HIS MADNESS	17
COMPLAINTS PROCEDURE	25
PUSSY	29
SMOG	37
JESMONDE	41
DUMPED?	47
THE BLACK DOG	51
MOBILE HOME	55

HORSEPLAY	61
TOP JUDGE	65
BEWITCHED	71
DUCKING THE QUESTION	75
BABY TALK	79
BIG EARS	83
ROUND ROBIN	89
ARE YOU COURTING?	95

PREFACE

This collection of short stories and skits is dedicated to the relatively small but obviously discerning group of people who read (or at least said they had read) my earlier collection. And in particular it is dedicated to the strikingly smaller number of them who asked for more.

For anyone who may inquire whether I have based any of the characters here on real people, the answer is No with the exception of three who are mentioned in newspaper extracts (one of whom remains unidentified, another is long deceased, and the third is probably in prison). All the others have come directly out of my imagination, and any resemblance to a person, living or dead, is genuinely and entirely coincidental. So it's not you, really it isn't, or anyone you know or thought you knew.

Happy reading!

Neil Butter.
London.
March 2010.

BURNING DESIRE
or THE SALAMANDER SYNDROME

"Funny thing, arson." My next door neighbour, a middle-aged barrister who spent his life defending criminals, had called in for what he liked to call a chat. He was wearing his usual well-worn black jacket and striped trousers, a throwback to an earlier age. He obviously modelled himself on Rumpole.

"How do you mean?"

"Well, it's not like other offences. Though it can be, for example when someone burns down their own factory so as to claim on the insurance. No, what interests me are those people who suffer from what I call the salamander syndrome."

"What on earth is that?"

My neighbour looked pleased. Another chance to display his vast knowledge of the world.

"I believe salamanders do exist but I mean the mythical creatures who are said to have lived in the middle of fire. You see, there are people who are fascinated by the whole thing. Harmless enough if they just get a thrill out of watching fireworks; the trouble comes when they feel a great urge to start a fire. For them it's such an excitement, they don't care about the consequences or the risk to other people."

"They must be mad."

"Ah, but how do you define madness? On one view of the matter, they are just irresponsible people who like their kicks."

"Well, they can enjoy their kicks as long as they don't come near here."

He laughed. "Don't worry. There aren't all that many of them around. Just my bad luck that the chap I was defending today didn't have much of a defence."

I could see there was no escape. "Just a moment. I'll go and get us both a drink." When I returned with the glasses, gin and tonic for me, whisky and water for him, my neighbour had settled himself even more comfortably into the armchair.

"So what was the defence?" I asked.

"It's an odd story. A man of good character who was found in possession of a box of matches."

"That sounds all right so far."

"Yes, but where do you think he was at the time?"

"I've no idea."

"Neither did he, according to him. He claimed he was suffering from a sudden bout of amnesia. But there's no doubt: he was on top of the roof of the local fire-station."

"Good grief! But what could he do with just a box of matches?"

My neighbour shifted uneasily. "Unfortunately, it wasn't just a box of matches. He had climbed up a ladder and at the foot of it was a large can of petrol. He said that this was another thing he knew nothing about."

"So what did he actually do?"

"Well, a fireman who had popped out for a quick cigarette looked up and saw my client lowering a piece of rope with a hook attached to it, towards the can."

"But if he was going to get the can, why wouldn't he just carry it up the ladder in the first place?"

"I'm glad you asked that. As a matter of fact, it was my best point but it didn't work."

"Why not?"

My neighbour gave a theatrical sigh. "The can of petrol was surprisingly heavy and carrying it up the ladder would have been even more difficult than hauling it up with a rope."

"Did your client give any explanation for having the rope? Or did he say it was all part of his amnesia?"

"He did have an explanation. He said that he always carried a piece of rope, ever since he was pushed over a cliff at the age of 10."

"What about the hook on the end?"

"He claimed that the police had planted it."

"But the fireman saw it."

"Yes; he said the fireman's eyesight must have been defective."

"I see what you mean when you say you didn't have much of a defence. On the other hand, when your client was caught he hadn't set fire to anything, had he?"

"No, he was only charged with an attempt. I argued that there was insufficient evidence to make him guilty of that but no-one agreed with me."

"Better luck next time."

"Thank you." He paused and sniffed the air a few times and then looked at me in surprise. "Is it my imagination or do I smell smoke?"

I chuckled. "No, it's not your imagination. You see, I didn't know about this salamander thing but what you were saying gave me a sort of burning desire. I've always been fascinated by fire, ever since the blanket on my bed went up in flames when I was a kid. So when I went to get the drinks a few minutes ago I took the liberty of starting a little bonfire in the kitchen."

He shot out of the chair. "Good God, you must be mad."

"Ah, but how do you define madness? Can I be your next client? As I have just said, better luck next time. Though of course it all depends upon us getting out of here alive."

He bolted out of the room towards the front door. I heard it slam after him.

A bit drastic of me, I reflected, as I moved the smoking frying pan to a safe place. But he was becoming such a bore and it was the best way of getting rid of him. Back in the sitting-room I settled down into the armchair. He had left some whisky in his glass. Pity to waste it. Somehow I didn't think he was likely to return.

Interesting though, what he had said about salamanders. I could see myself getting hooked on them one day. Of course that rubbish about the blanket going up in flames wasn't true but I could just imagine the thrill of a big fire. The surreptitious match. The initial spark, then a few shafts of flame, then a crackle as the flames began to catch hold, then within minutes a positive roar as they surged upwards and merged with the sight and choking smell of smoke and burning wood. And the smoke getting greater and greater and greater until it smothered everything within its grasp! And the heat getting stronger and stronger and stronger until there was a final blaze of destruction! When water and foam and all the resources available to man fought a losing battle! When in the end there was nothing left except smouldering carnage and debris and ruin! Oh yes, yes, yes!

I was trembling like a leaf; the glass fell from my hand; my mouth had gone dry. I don't know why.

Funny thing, arson.

PEARLY GATES

Saint Peter sat irritably at the Pearly Gates looking down at the figure struggling up the long ladder. Of course the chap had had a nasty coronary very recently but even so he was making heavy weather of the climb. And the Relief Saint ought to have come and taken over half-an-hour ago and still hadn't put in an appearance. Typical!

Saint Peter consulted the sheets of paper on his clipboard. There were far too many blank spaces in the information columns. One simply couldn't get the staff these days. But at least the sheets were in the right order. The man climbing up the ladder was Mervyn, and the Vetting Committee had said that it would be all right for him to enter subject to the usual routine questions. And here he was at last.

"Mervyn, isn't it?"

"Yes, are you who I think you are?"

"Probably. I understand you have spent a couple of days in Purgatory. Not too bad, I trust?"

"No worse than the office I worked in for fifteen years."

Peter consulted the clipboard again. "Ah yes, I see you were an income tax inspector in Swansea. Do you mind if I ask you a few questions? Purely routine."

"No, carry on."

"Have you in the past worshipped any idols?"

"No, though I did use to have a thing about Cliff Richard when I was much younger."

Peter ticked the tick-box. "That's okay, join the club. Did you normally observe the Sabbath?"

"Yes, indeed. I watched television most of the day."

Peter inserted a half-tick. "Did you honour and respect your father and mother?"

"My father went AWOL soon after I was born having apparently told my Mum I was an ugly little brat so I can't really say I respected or honoured him. But my Mum, that's a different matter. I positively worshipped the ground she trod on. She was the most marvellous person. When I think of all she did for me ...."

"Yes, yes," Peter said hurriedly. "I get the picture. I'm sure you haven't committed murder, so I will skip that one, but what about adultery?"

There was a moment's pause. "No," Mervyn said.

Peter glanced again at the clip-board. This was one area where the staff were surprisingly efficient. "What about the brunette who used to work for you?"

"Oh yes, now you mention it. But it was only two or three times after the Christmas office party."

"And what about Maureen?"

"Good Heavens! I had entirely forgotten about her. That was a long time ago, you know, though I do remember she was pretty stunning."

"Theft?"

"No, certainly not, apart from a spot of shop-lifting when I was aged about eleven."

"Have you coveted your neighbour's ox?"

"No, he never had one. He had an old Land Rover."

There were further questions which, strictly speaking, Peter should have asked but he was getting bored. "Okay, that will do nicely. You're in."

"Thanks very much. It's quite a relief."

Mervyn started to pass through the Gates.

"Hold on a moment," Peter observed. "The next person coming up is someone you know."

Mervyn looked down. "Good Heavens!" he said for the second time. "It's Maureen. I had no idea. What on earth happened to her?"

The clip-board came in useful. "Nasty road accident," Peter explained. "But she seems to have lead a pretty blameless life apart from er...... one or two incidents many years ago, so you will probably be able to renew your er...... acquaintanceship with her soon."

"But what an extraordinary coincidence that she should be following directly behind me."

"Not entirely. We try to keep prospective entrants in some sort of alphabetical order. We don't always manage it, of course. Terrible trouble with our P's and Q's only last week."

"Oh I see, but do you mind if I make myself scarce? I don't feel quite up to meeting her just yet."

Mervyn disappeared through the Gates.

Maureen had almost reached the top of the ladder. Saint Peter looked appraisingly at her. Goodness me, he said to himself. She's really got something. And I thought I had lost interest in that sort of thing years ago.

He leant down solicitously. "Maureen, isn't it?"

"Yes. Are you Saint Peter?"

"Got it in one. But if you like, just call me Pete."

"Thanks, Pete. You know, it's odd but I thought I recognised that man ahead of me."

"Maybe, but you can always see him later. He's not up to much at the moment. As a matter of fact, I ought to be asking you a few questions but we can stuff that for a lark because I have got a better idea."

"Like what?"

"Need you ask?"

"Do you really mean that? After all, we hardly know each other."

"Of course I mean it. Do I look like the sort of bloke who goes around making suggestions of that kind to everyone?"

"No, you don't. Oh, all right then. After all, we've only got one life."

"Well that's arguable, but there is a question I need to ask: your place or mine?"

THE WEDDING TOAST

He stood, unsteadily, a glass in his hand.

"Ladies and gentlemen, in a few moments I will propose a toast to the Bride and Groom though I may not last that long because as you can probably see I am pissed out of my mind. As most of you know, I am not the father but one step up or one step down, take your choice, yes the step-father. So I'm the lucky chap who has to pay the bill for all this. And you've guessed it, that explains why we are drinking sparkling-wine rather than proper fizz. Not that Emily's real dad would have done any better because he's a mean bastard and I for one am glad he's not here. Okay, okay, let bygones be bygones, whatever that may mean.

"So what is a step-father meant to say on these occasions? God knows. What I can say is that Emily is a great girl. She first came into my orbit, if that's the right word, six years ago when she was just twelve. I don't think she liked me very much, all right, all right, I know what you are thinking, and then when her Mum and me really got together, she couldn't bear the sight of me. I can't say I blame her. But it was a difficult time for all of us. Do you mind if I have another quick swig?

"Then, much later, it all changed, I can't really say why. Well, for whatever reason, me and her Mum weren't hitting it off as well as we had hoped, and I can remember now, come to think of it, the very day it all changed. It was a hot Saturday in late June, one of those brilliant days, you know, we sometimes get in England. Emily was fifteen, nearly sixteen, and the two of us went out into the country for a picnic together as her Mum was doing something else, visiting poor Aunt Kitty I seem to remember. We had a few glasses of wine, and well, as I've said, she was nearly sixteen and it was a hot day and what with one thing and another it just happened. And of course it has gone on happening, from time to time. Oh! Aunt Priss, you sour-faced old bitch, for God's sake stop looking so sodding disapproving, just because you've never had it away with anybody throughout your entire life doesn't mean that you can go around with a face creased like an elephant's backside. Sorry, I didn't mean it, not about the backside anyway.

"So when six months ago, this bright young man - okay, okay, you may not recognise the description - but I mean the Groom, started going out with my beloved Emily, I was in a state of despair. Another quick swig if you don't mind. Then came the news that she was pregnant. She doesn't go in for condoms and the Pill doesn't suit her, so I suppose it was almost bound to happen. Who is the father? She doesn't seem to know, and of course these days there is no need to get married. Saves a lot of money on the wedding if you don't. But she was quite determined to go ahead and since obviously I couldn't marry her and, fair's fair, there's an age gap of over thirty years between us, she decided to marry this young man. So that's why we are all here, sod it!

"So from my point of view, this is the worst day of my life. But I mustn't spoil your day, dearest Emily, or for that matter spoil the day for any of the rest of you gormless turds, and please forgive me because I am starting to cry. Oh God! I didn't mean it to be like this. Just one more swig. All I can say is that I wish this young couple all the happiness in the world, even though I think the whole thing is a sodding disaster. How could you do this to me, Emily darling, and when can I, you know, see you again? Oh shit! I think I am going to fall over. No, don't worry, I'll manage this last bit somehow. Do you mind if I blow my nose?

"Sorry everybody. I think I have said enough, some of you may think more than enough, but anyway for the few of you who aren't so totally pissed you can't even stand, I ask you to rise and drink a toast. The Bride and Groom."

He studied himself in the mirror. Not a pretty sight. Maudlin and half-cut. Later he would have to rehearse his speech again for the wedding tomorrow. But it did need a few changes, even he could see that.

DILEMMAS

"Sorry to trouble you but I need someone to come and change a wheel."

At the other end of the helpline, the female operator sighed. Why couldn't motorists manage to change their own stupid wheels instead of calling for help, like little children asking for Mummy?

"Certainly, sir," she said smoothly. "I just need your membership number, particulars of the vehicle and your exact location."

Daniel supplied the information, including the location near Regent's Park, and then sat in the car drumming his fingers impatiently on the dashboard. Fifty minutes later, a brightly-coloured rescue van drew up and a cheerful young man emerged and introduced himself as Gerry.

"Got a puncture, have we?" he inquired, looking at the completely flat tyre. "No worries: if you've got a spare I can change it in a jiff."

"Yes, I've got a good spare in the boot."

Gerry jacked the car up, removed the offending wheel, and opened the boot. As he was about to lift out the spare wheel he noticed something odd. Immediately beneath it there was a strange-looking package, about 14 inches by 10, covered in brown paper, torn at one end. Gerry checked that Daniel was out of sight, cautiously eased it out of its hiding place, and leant forward to sniff it. His suspicions were confirmed: unless he was much mistaken, there was a distinct smell of cannabis (which he happened to be familiar with). Personally he didn't disapprove but the sheer amount here must be enormous, probably worth thousands.

Oh, hell! What a dilemma! Should he just ignore it and pretend he was one of the Three Wise Monkeys? It would look bad if he shopped a customer but as against that he had touched the wretched package and his own slightly greasy fingerprints were probably on it. Should he try to wipe them off or would part of his DNA somehow stick? No time to think. He reached a decision.

"Won't be a sec." he called out to Daniel who was sitting reading a newspaper on a low brick wall nearby. "Just have to make a quick call to headquarters." He walked a few paces away so as to be out of earshot before dialling 999 on his mobile. He explained the situation urgently. "Give us 10 minutes," he was told, "And we'll be with you."

Ten minutes. It should be enough though he now rather regretted his earlier reference to "a jiff". He returned to the car and pretended to have difficulty in removing the spare wheel and getting it into place. "You've got stiff hub caps," he explained conversationally. The car was still jacked up when the roar of police sirens cut through the air and two police cars shot into sight and screeched to a halt.

Four young police officers leapt out, quivering with the eagerness of foxhounds about to sink their teeth into their prey.

Gerry silently indicated the package.

"Is this your car, sir?" one of the young officers asked the white-faced Daniel. He nodded. "And how did this come to be in the boot?" Daniel said nothing; he just shook his head.

"In that case I am arresting you on suspicion of being in possession of a class B drug with intent to supply............."

Three other police cars screeched up. The officers sitting inside saw that the situation was rather obviously under control but lingered hopefully for a few minutes before roaring away on some other mission.

~~~~~~~~~~~~~~~

Two weeks later the Superior Officer sat at his desk as he gave the young arresting officer a bollocking.

"You know what the Lab has come up with, don't you? No skunk or pot or anything illegal, just camel shit. Pure camel shit! I can hardly believe it. Half of our lads chased across north London, all for the sake of a bit of camel shit. We've been made to look like stupid pricks, so what have you to say?"

"With respect, sir, I didn't know the man worked at the zoo and I wasn't to know it was camel shit. We had received a radio call saying there was a large packet of cannabis in the boot so naturally I assumed that's what it was."

"You assumed. You assumed. Couldn't you see it was only camel shit?"

"No, sir, I'm afraid not. It was in a package and anyway I can't say I have ever seen camel shit before, at least not at close range. Couldn't we just get the man for nicking it from the zoo?"

The Superior Officer gave a superior smile. "No joy. We asked the blokes at the zoo. They said they didn't care a ......, well I won't tell you exactly what they said, but the effect was that he ought to have got permission but the stuff is almost worthless and if he wants it as fertiliser for his garden he's welcome to it. So all I can say is, don't let this happen again."

"No, sir, though if you don't mind me saying so, I wouldn't expect to come across this situation all that often."

At about the same time, back at home, Daniel was re-reading the official letter in his hand: no further action against him was intended. Stupid of him to have left that package in the boot; he had entirely forgotten about it, part of a scam he had carried out months ago. But thank God the police hadn't searched his car properly and discovered the false compartment in the back seat where he stashed away the hard drugs. He could hardly believe his luck. All the same, the whole experience had been a terrible shock. If they had found the real stuff, he would have been sent down for years. In fact the more he thought about it, the more his hands shook. Yes, he was losing his grip in every sense of the word. Was this the moment of truth: had the time come to stop dealing altogether? Dilemma! Yes, no, yes, no, yes, no. Yes, final decision: it was time to stop.

So - as well as all their valuable work in the desert - camels clearly have their uses.

METHOD IN HIS MADNESS

Across the large desk, the Harley Street psychiatrist scrutinised his new patient Oliver. There was something strange about the man. He could be a merchant banker or a partner in a City firm of solicitors, but this didn't tie in with the red thatch of hair, possibly a toupee, plus the matching goatee beard. The man had in fact described himself as an unsuccessful writer, the author of eleven novels, only one of which had been published, and of two books of verse, neither of which had found a publisher. (*Marginal note: low self-esteem?*)

The psychiatrist cleared his throat. "Unusually, I don't seem to have received a letter of referral from your GP so I want to check the history which you have just given me? Right?"

Oliver nodded.

"You were born in Kenya, the only son of a Welsh civil engineer and an Irish mother, and are now fifty-three. Because of some sort of scandal, your parents had to flee from Mombassa and so they brought you to England at the age of five. You always had problems relating to your peers and tended to be a solitary child, spending much of your time playing card games with yourself and also playing the flute. Right?"

"Right."

"At school you were frequently bullied which you attribute to your er..... protruding ears. You were poor at sport though on one occasion you scored eleven runs at cricket. The figure eleven has been important to you ever since. You were subject to depressive episodes from the age of six until fourteen; as I mentioned, this is relatively unusual for someone so young. From the age of fifteen you experienced anxiety attacks which were associated with your belief that dinosaurs were about to invade England and attack you. (*psychotic? paranoic?*) Right?"

"Right."

"When you left school you joined the police force because you felt that this was the best way of getting protection in respect of dinosaurs. You soon became disillusioned, however, and went to work with a firm of publishers specialising in children's illustrated books. Within a few months, for reasons which you are unable to explain, your fears about dinosaurs abated and you now accept - very realistically if I may say so - that dinosaurs are entirely extinct. Right?"

"Right."

"In due course, you decided to become a writer; you were able to afford this because you were then living with a wealthy and supportive Brazilian woman. Unhappily, after three years she left you and went to live with a bi-sexual social worker in Berwick-upon-Tweed. You have come to see me because you are increasingly aware of short-term memory-losses and you are concerned that you may be developing some form of dementia. (*possible but unlikely at this age.*) Right?"

"Right."

"Well now, I may decide in due course that it would be prudent for you to undergo certain specific er.... procedures but first I want to carry out a few simple tests myself. All right?"

"Yes, right."

"Let's start with something fairly basic: what day of the week is it?"

Oliver paused. "Tuesday, I think," he said cautiously.

"Very close; actually it's Thursday. What month is it?"

Another pause. "September?"

"Again close; it's October. What year is it?"

A long pause. "1893?"

"Oh dear, no. We are well into the twenty-first century. What made you say 1893?"

"It's just a year that seems to have stuck in my mind."

"Right. Let's change tack. What is the name of the Prime Minister?"

This time the answer came without a moment's hesitation. "William Gladstone."

The psychiatrist coughed discreetly. "Let's look at it in another way. I want you to concentrate on the present if you can but please don't feel under any sort of pressure. So, let me ask: how did you get to my consulting room this morning?"

"I walked."

"No question of driving a car or using a bus or the Tube?"

"No."

"I raised that because you told me earlier that you live in Potters Bar. It just struck me that it must be a remarkably long walk. Do you think you may simply have forgotten your mode of transport?"

"No, I walked."

"Right. Let's change tack again. Tell me your mother's maiden name."

The reply came slowly. "I don't remember. I never knew her very well."

"It's my fault: I should have started by taking a full family history. What er….. happened?"

Oliver spoke blankly. "She died, she was killed, I was only six at the time."

"I am very sorry to hear that. When you say *killed*, er….. how did that happen? Was it a motor accident?"

Oliver looked down at the floor. "No, nothing like that"

The psychiatrist waited, pen raised. *Best to let the man explain himself.*

The voice was subdued. "I still find it difficult to talk about. She went back to Kenya for a safari with some friends. She was mauled to death by a lion. I wasn't there of course but I often think of it. It was ghastly, ghastly." Oliver buried his head in his hands.

"How absolutely appalling! I am really sorry. Here, use one of these Kleenex tissues. Even though you weren't there, a traumatic event like that could I suppose explain your depressive episodes when you were a child. Who subsequently looked after you? Was it just your father?"

"Him and my Aunt Molly. It was a terrible time of my life. We all lived in Wales."

"Did you and your aunt not get on well?"

"No, I hated her: she drank heavily, you know."

"Are you suggesting that - perhaps under the influence of drink - she became abusive in some way?"

"I can't say that she did. She just sulked in a corner. Though now you mention it, she did throw saucepans and suchlike at my Dad from time to time."

"Was your father a drinker as well?"

"Not really. Only on the Sabbath."

"I'm trying to get a picture of your life at that time. Looking back on it, what do you feel was the real source of your unhappiness?"

"Welsh sheep."

"I beg your pardon?"

"Welsh sheep. We just never saw eye to eye."

"I assume you lived on a farm?"

"No, we lived in Merthyr Tydfil."

"I'm not sure that I fully understand all this but I suggest we break off for the time being. Obviously you have given me a lot of extremely useful material but frankly it does require some thought on my part. I will have to work out a plan of action for our next meeting."

"How often will we need to meet? When can I expect some form of closure?"

The psychiatrist looked up sharply from his notes. "*Closure?* That's a word we come across in my profession. Have you experienced any previous psychiatric er….. intervention?"

"No, it's just a word I use in some of my novels. I also use the word <u>pickaxe</u> a lot. Nothing wrong with that, is there?"

What an odd man, completely bizarre. Leave it for the time being.

"No, I'm sure not. Well, I'm afraid I can't say at present how many more consultations will be necessary but shall we meet at the same time, same day, er…. Thursday you remember, next week? Perhaps you would be kind enough to write out a cheque now while I jot down a few more notes? I believe my secretary has told you what my fees are."

The two men wrote industriously.

Oliver passed his cheque over the desk.

The psychiatrist glanced at it for a few moments, then he blanched visibly. After an appreciable pause, he said slowly and with an obvious effort, "I am not too troubled about the day and the month but my bank is hardly going to accept a cheque dated 1893. And I think you know perfectly well that my name is not Doctor Robespierre, and although my fees are hardly trivial I suspect that you also know that I do not charge eleven thousand pounds for a single consultation. And what do you mean by signing yourself as *The Mad Hatter?*"

The men stared silently at each other.

Then the psychiatrist spoke in a dry tightly-controlled voice. "I had thought that this was the first of several consultations but I am now driven to the conclusion that it is also our last. Right?"

"Right," said Oliver, rising rapidly and shooting out of the room, past the surprised secretary and out of the front door. He sprinted down Harley Street and turned into a nearby mews. Nobody tried to follow him. He pulled off the toupee and the false beard and stuffed them into his jacket pocket. He glanced at his watch: it was not yet ten o'clock.

Shortly afterwards he walked sedately through the front entrance of a building rather similar to the one he had just left.

His secretary gave him a bright smile. "'Morning, doctor. Your new patient is here already. Shall I give you a few minutes?"

"Yes, please." He entered his consulting room and sat down behind the large desk.

He began to chuckle. It had of course been a barmy thing to do but the chances of detection were slight. He had long ago ceased to attend those expensive and slightly absurd conventions so favoured by psychiatrists (understandably located in exotic cities like San Francisco and Marrakesh) so the chances of meeting the other man were remote. If they happened to pass each other in the street, the absence of the toupee and beard should do the trick. If spoken to, he would assume a thick guttural accent in a strange foreign tongue. And the cheque he had used was from an old account with a bank which no longer existed.

The highlight of the whole thing had been the psychiatrist's expression as he was taking the extraordinary history and in particular when he was told the terrible fate of Oliver's mother (in fact still alive and living happily in Sidcup, if that wasn't a contradiction in terms). It had been well worth the risk. Anyway, it was always fun to see how other members of the profession dealt with er….. problems.

There was a discreet knock at the door. Oliver rose and extended a welcoming outstretched hand to the patient who was ushered in. Then he took a sudden astonished step backwards. There wasn't much doubt about it: the man looked exactly like a small dinosaur.

For a brief moment, Oliver wondered if he himself needed psychiatric help. But he made an immediate diagnosis. No, of course not! There was nothing wrong with him. He just had an exceptionally good imagination.

Seated at the desk, he studied the GP's letter in front of him and then looked up at his patient. He switched on his reassuring professional voice and manner.

"I will have to take a full history from you," he explained. "You see, your doctor's letter only deals with the last couple of years. I'm afraid we will have to go back further. Much further. In fact, several million years …….."

COMPLAINTS PROCEDURE

Mrs Hetherington the head-teacher sat at her desk looking contentedly through the window of her room towards the flower-beds immediately outside. It was nearly midday and, most unusually, she had been able to get on with the necessary administration free of interruption. Long may this continue, she reflected.

At that moment, the 'phone rang. Her secretary spoke in a hushed whisper. "I'm afraid it's Mrs Snodd. She says it's urgent."

The head-teacher groaned inwardly. Mrs Snodd, the mother of Diana a spiteful girl of thirteen with bad breath, was a constant thorn in the flesh.

"All right, put her through."

"It's a disgrace, a complete disgrace. Call yourself a school. And what are you doing about it? Nothing, I suppose."

"What is the problem?"

"Problem! You call it a problem? Sheer favouritism, that's what it is, and my poor Diana comes out worst every time."

The head-teacher sighed and dropped a crumb from the remains of a cheese-sandwich into the waste-paper basket. Heaven knows, it was difficult enough dealing with over three hundred adolescent boys and girls but most of them were positive saints compared with the parents.

"As you know, there is an official complaints procedure so I suggest you put your complaint into writing and I will of course consider the matter carefully in due course."

There was a crackle of indignation at the other end of the 'phone. "Oh no, I know your sort. Take the easy way out if you can. Me and Mr Snodd are going to come and see you whether you like it or not. So there!"

Mrs Hetherington gave another sigh. If only I had a stun-gun, she thought, preferably one which could be fired through the telephone.

"Very well, of course I will see you. About four-thirty on Thursday? I look forward to it."

They arrived twenty minutes late. Mrs Snodd was a little woman, badly dressed and quivering with anger. Her husband followed a few paces behind. He wore a cheap pin-striped suit and a mouse-coloured moustache which somehow matched his constant sniff.

Mrs Snodd launched into a tirade.

"I know my rights. We didn't get our Diana into this school, and I may say we had a lot of trouble doing it, just for her to be picked on and humiliated, yes humiliated, there's no other word, and all because of that wretched woman who's not fit enough to run a fish-and-chip shop, let alone a class of teenage boys and girls."

The head-teacher raised a hand to stop the flood.

"Can we just try to get the facts clear? I assume you are referring to Diana's class-teacher. In what specific way are you saying that she has picked on and humiliated your daughter?"

Mrs Snodd gave a loud snort, which was accompanied by an equally loud sniff from her husband.

"Favouritism, that's what it is. And all at the expense of my poor Diana."

Mrs Snodd produced a large mauve handkerchief as though to wipe away an improbable tear.

Mrs Hetherington stretched out a hand for her imaginary stun-gun.

"I still want to know what specific complaint you are making. Give me an example of the favouritism."

"I'll give you an example all right. Last week all the class handed in a piece of written work. And do you know what? Our Diana came second from bottom. Second from bottom! And she's a bright girl, make no mistake. Don't tell me that's not favouritism. What do you say, Fred?"

Mr Snodd gave a loud sniff and nodded obediently. "That was favouritism all right. Stands to reason."

Mrs Hetherington firmly pulled the trigger. "Has it occurred to you that on this occasion her work just happened to be poorer than the rest of the class?"

Mrs Snodd gave a roar of anger. "That is EXACTLY, EXACTLY, what I thought you would say. Who's side are you on? Not the parents, that's for sure. You lot all stick together, that's your trouble or one of your troubles. Sick, I call it."

"I'm sorry you should express yourself in that way," the head-teacher said smoothly, wondering at the same time whether it was okay to go on pulling the trigger or whether stun-guns had to be reloaded somehow. "But I will tell you what I will do. Either I or my deputy will check the marks to see whether your daughter has been treated unfairly and I will let you know the result."

"That's a fat lot of good," said Mrs Snodd, rising to her feet. "I don't trust you or anybody else in this place, as you well know and for good reason. Come on, Fred, we're wasting our time here. We'll have the Law on you, Mrs Pleased With Yourself. We're not standing for this. It's a disgrace."

Nearly a week passed without another word from the Snodds though Diana continued to attend school. Then at about eleven o'clock one morning, the 'phone rang on Mrs Hetherington's desk. The secretary spoke in a hushed whisper. "I'm afraid it's Mrs Snodd. She says it's urgent."

The head-teacher groaned. "All right, put her through."

The raucous voice at the other end was almost incandescent with rage. "It's a disgrace, a complete disgrace. Your staff have been getting at my poor Diana again."

The head-teacher sighed. "I suppose there is no point in my asking you to follow our complaints procedure?"

"Too true, there isn't. You know what you can do with your sodding complaints procedure. Me and Mr Snodd are going to come and see you again, and this time we want some action IF you don't mind."

"I could fit you in tomorrow afternoon at four-fifteen. All right? Fine."

Mrs Hetherington put down the 'phone and gazed thoughtfully into space. Something drastic was called for. But what? Then she had an idea. The religious education teacher happened to be married to, or at least living with, a very senior police officer. That could be useful. She picked up the intercom.

"Sorry to trouble you. Rather an unusual request. Could you get hold of a stun-gun for me by tomorrow afternoon?........ Yes, a real one.......... Why? Oh, I am just reviewing the complaints procedure....... Yes, it needs to be made more effective. One way or another."

PUSSY

My dear Charles,

As you know, I have always admired and respected you as a next door neighbour and I hope you will forgive me if I mention that in recent times your cat, who I believe is imaginatively called Pussy, has been a source of exasperation to Margaret and myself. The problem is that during the day-time she seems to assume that she (I am of course referring to Pussy) can treat our garden as though it were her own and, further, in the early hours of many mornings she either indulges in passionate love affairs or conducts ferocious fights. The noise has often seriously interfered with our sleep-pattern.

I apologise for troubling you but I wonder if you could deal with these matters?

With warmest regards,

Yours ever,

Matthew

My dear Mathew,
I am naturally sorry to receive your letter concerning Pussy.
I too have always enjoyed our friendly relationship but what exactly are you asking me to do?
Kind regards,
Charles

My dear Charles,
Thank you for your letter. With all due respect, it is your cat and surely it is for you to exercise the necessary amount of control. Precisely how you achieve this is a matter for you.
Regards,
Matthew

Dear Matthew,
Thank you for your letter. I know of no way in which I can explain to Pussy that she should not enter your garden. You are, however, welcome to buy a cat-deterrent of the sort which emits a high pitch noise when it detects the presence of a cat; so far as I know this does not cause any physical harm to the animal in question.
Charles

Dear Charles,
Thank you but I have no wish to incur the expense which you suggest and which in any event I suspect would not be effective in relation to cats like Pussy. I note that you have not dealt with the nocturnal problem. Is there any reason why you don't keep your cat locked up at night?
Matthew

Dear Matthew,
I take exception to your comment "in relation to cats like Pussy". What are you implying? As to what you describe as the nocturnal problem, I happen to have strong views about imprisonment and have no intention of locking Pussy up.
Charles

Charles,
I just happen to think that, very much like yourself, Pussy is too strong-willed to be deterred by anything at all. I should place on record that I think your reference to imprisonment is ludicrous; for all I know, Pussy would be perfectly happy to spend a few hours indoors at night-time.
Matthew

Matthew,
How the hell do you know what my Pussy wants to do at night-time? I can only think that you are sex-starved or otherwise you would have more sympathy with her love-life.
Charles

Charles,
I am sorry you see fit to descend into the gutter; I may add that Margaret also takes strong exception to your comments. I have no doubt
that you seriously believe that, in addition to her love-life, your wretched cat enjoys her frequent fights at night.
Matthew

Matthew,
Yes, I think it's more than possible that she enjoys a bit of rough; I need hardly say that I object to your description of her.
Charles

Charles, In view of your attitude, I am putting the matter into the hands of my Solicitors. Matthew

Matthew, I always thought you were a little turd and now I know.
Charles

Talking of turds, Charles, would you like to look into our garden and see what your beloved Pussy has just done? Matthew

Dear Sir,
Re: Pussy
We have been consulted by your neighbour Matthew in relation to the unhappy dispute involving your Pussy.
It is clear that the activities of the cat constitute a nuisance and if this persists we have instructions to issue injunction proceedings against you.
Our client has no wish to take this course and we must ask for your undertaking that you will take all reasonable steps to abate the nuisance.
Yours faithfully,
Handlebroom, Munching, Fox and Webb, Solicitors

Dear Sirs,
Thank you for your letter concerning Pussy.
What exactly are you asking me to do?
Faithfully Yours.
Charles.

Dear Sir,
Re: Pussy
Thank you for your letter.
With all due respect, it is your cat and it is for you to exercise the necessary amount of control. Precisely how you achieve this is a matter for you.
Yours faithfully,
Handlebroom, Munching, Fox and Webb, Solicitors.

Dear Sirs,
Here we go again.
Tell your client to get a cat-deterrent.
Faithfully Yours.
Charles.

Dear Sir,
Re: Pussy
Thank you for your letter.
Our client has no wish to incur the expense which you suggest.
We continue to await your undertaking.
Yours faithfully,
Handlebroom, Munching, Fox and Webb, Solicitors.

Dear Sirs,
Surely your fees are going to be far in excess of the cost of a cat-deterrent?
Faithfully Yours,
Charles

Dear Sir,
Re: Pussy
Thank you for your letter.
We have no intention of discussing our fees with you.
Please give us the undertaking we require.
Yours faithfully,
Handlebroom, Munching, Fox and Webb, Solicitors.

Dear Sir,
Re: Pussy
We are concerned that we have not heard from you for some time.
We await your undertaking.
Yours faithfully,
Handlebroom, Munching, Fox and Webb, Solicitors.

Dear Sirs,

I now feel able to give you the undertaking which you require - without prejudice to my contention that your requirement is a load of codswallop - because some weeks ago Pussy departed and has not been seen since. It is of course possible that she will return but I think this is unlikely in view of the fact that I have just bought two Rottweilers. This purchase should eliminate the possibility of complaints by your client concerning his garden but in fairness I should mention that both dogs have an exceptionally loud bark. I look forward to hearing from you, above the noise of barking, in due course. For your reference, I have (in your honour) named the dogs respectively Munching and Fox. (I confess that I thought of calling one of them "Handlebroom" but I decided that this would be a silly name for a Rottweiler.) Perhaps you would be good enough to head any further correspondence with their names on the same principle that your letters have previously been headed "Re: Pussy".
Faithfully Yours,
Charles

Dear Sir,
<u>Re: Pussy and Rottweilers</u>
We acknowledge receipt of your letter and accept your undertaking concerning Pussy although this now seems to be otiose; we should place on record our distaste at your choice of language.
As to the dogs, we must ask you to let us have your undertaking to take all reasonable steps to avoid any nuisance which may arise out of their barking.
Yours faithfully,
Handlebroom, Munching, Fox and Webb, Solicitors.

Dear Sirs,
What exactly are you asking me to do?
Faithfully Yours,
Charles

Dear Sir,
Re: Rottweilers
Shit! Here we go again. Why don't we all stop farting about?
Yours etc.

Note from Susie to Mr Handlebroom: this is what I would like to say but I realise you will want me to draft something rather more formal! I'll make sure that no letter goes out until I have discussed it with you.

Note from Susie to Mr Handlebroom: terribly sorry, I'm afraid the temp secretary typed it and sent it out as above. What can we do to prevent ourselves being reported to the Law Society?

Dear Sirs,
Thank you for your admirable letter.
I agree wholeheartedly with the sentiments expressed in it.
Let's call it a day. And what a fitting end to this long saga!
Faithfully Yours,
Charles

Note from Susie to Mr Handlebroom: Do we need to reply?

Mr Handlebroom to Susie: No. By the way, have you still got Pussy safely locked up?

SMOG

London, November 1950.

Stanley edged his black taxi slowly eastwards along Fleet Street, cursing the smog which hung like a malevolent spirit over the whole City. It was a cold evening, visibility was just about zilch, and the heavy, yellow poisoned air tugged at his chest. And it had been a bad day for trade with only a handful of customers, none of whom had been generous with their tips.

He was passing Ye Olde Cheshire Cheese which dated back centuries when he heard a shout. "Cab!" In the gloom, Stanley could make out the outline of a tall man wearing a long black cloak. Cautiously he brought the taxi to a halt.

"Highgate Hill, near the top, if you please." The voice was that of a gentleman, deep and with authority.

"Very well, sir." But Stanley groaned to himself. Good to have another customer of course but oh God! *Highgate* where the smog might just become plain fog but where visibility would be even worse.

As Stanley turned left at Ludgate Circus, the passenger leant forward and slid back the glass a few inches. "This is a nice conveyance."

Conveyance indeed! " I'm glad you like it, sir."

"Have you had it long?" Clearly the man wanted a chat.

"Just over a year, sir. This is the second cab I have bought. On hire-purchase of course."

"What is hire-purchase?"

Jesus! Some mothers do have them. A quick look at the interior mirror merely revealed a shadowy figure in the back. "Oh, haven't you come across it, sir? It's a way of buying something but you pay by instalments."

"How ingenious! And can you buy anything with this hire-purchase?"

"Just about, sir."

The man seemed satisfied with the exchange and sat back in silence for a few minutes.

But Stanley was intrigued. "Do you often do this journey, sir?"

"Only on the rare occasions I travel down to the City."

"So you normally stay in Highgate?"

"Yes, it's not the sort of journey one wants to make every day."

"I suppose not, sir," said Stanley, thinking of the thousands of commuters who did just that. "But with the Tube, it doesn't take very long, does it?"

"I am not familiar with that. I prefer the horse and carriage."

Ye Gods and Little Fishes, as Stanley's father used to say in times of crisis. Was the man a nut-case on his way back to a loony-bin in Highgate? And even though he might be a gent, what were the chances of a decent tip from him at the end? If they ever got there.

Stanley kept to the main roads where the movement of traffic helped to disperse the smog. Though only slightly. Despite the cold, a trickle of perspiration trickled down his forehead: he couldn't remember worse conditions, not ever.

Now they were travelling slowly up the Holloway Road. The tail lights of the car in front disappeared. A traffic light loomed up immediately ahead, already turning red. Stanley braked heavily. There was a thud from the back of the cab.

He looked round anxiously. "Are you all right, sir?"

There was a muffled chuckle. "Perfectly all right, my good man. I should have been hanging on more tightly. Pray continue."

Not while there's a red light against me, Stanley said to himself, I suppose you have never heard of traffic lights. But in a few moments the green came on and Stanley eased forward.

As the taxi began to climb Highgate Hill, the engine started to labour.

"Not enough horse-power," Stanley explained apologetically over his shoulder.

He sensed the man's surprise. "Not enough *what*?"

"Horse-power."

"But my dear fellow, this is extraordinary. Where are the horses?"

Was he trying to be funny? "It's nothing to do with horses as you may know them, sir. It's a way of measuring engine-power."

"What a very curious expression."

Now the smog had lost some of its yellow tint and, as anticipated, was more like a conventional fog. The taxi continued up the hill. Stanley waited for instructions.

"Take the next turning to the left, and stop the carriage after twenty yards."

Carriage! Clearly a nutter. I'll be glad when this is all over. Stanley slowed down yet further, spotted the junction just in time, turned left and stopped as directed.

He looked at the meter. "That will be……." He broke off, suddenly aware that the rear of the cab was empty. There had been no sound of a door opening or shutting.

He switched off the engine and cautiously got out. The road was empty. No sign or sound of life, apart from the muted noise of traffic from Highgate Hill. So, remarkably, the man had done a runner. No fare, no tip. And, despite the voice, obviously no gentleman but a complete……. Stanley mouthed an obscenity.

He opened a rear door and the light came on. Something was glittering on the seat. Two solid gold sovereigns! Carefully he picked them up, studied them, and placed them in his jacket pocket. What was their value? He had no idea, but it must be at least ten times more than the fare.

Slowly and thoughtfully he climbed back into the driver's seat and was about to start the engine when he paused. What was that odd sound? It seemed to be coming directly out of the fog and was rushing towards him, louder and louder. In God's name, what could it be? Yes, it must be, it couldn't be anything else: it was the sound of horses' hooves.

He started up, slammed the cab into gear, and without a backward glance accelerated fiercely into the fog and towards the City's smog.

At least he would feel safer there.

JESMONDE

I'm Miles and I am twelve years old and I am in love with my school teacher Miss Feather. She is quite old, thirty at least, so I suppose there is not much hope.

I am tall for my age and she is short and stocky but she has a nice nose and a nice smile. What I really go for is that she treats me like an equal and doesn't talk down to me like snot-face Mrs Treadwinter and most of the other teachers, come to think of it.

We live near each other so we sometimes walk back homewards after school. One day last week she unexpectedly said to me, "Would you like to come in for a cup of tea or an orange juice? I've got some Jaffa cakes as well."

"Yes, please," I said, surprised. It would be interesting to see what sort of place she lived in. And I liked Jaffa cakes.

"There's someone I want you to meet."

We turned into a side street and stopped outside a large terraced house. "It's nothing very grand," she said apologetically, "so don't expect too much."

"It looks very grand to me," I commented, glancing up at the smart-looking house with little balconies outside the windows.

"Oh, I only live in a small part of it." She went ahead down some steps to the basement area and opened the front door with her keys. "Come in."

It was a small, rather dark flat or apartment or whatever and although it was very clean there was a faint whiff of some sort of animal.

"Make yourself at home in the front room and I will get something from the kitchen. Tea or orange juice?"

I hated tea and didn't much like orange juice but as she hadn't offered coke or pepsi I asked for juice.

Just as I was looking at a photograph on the mantelpiece of someone who more-or-less resembled Miss Feather as she might have been ninety years ago there was a loud cry of horror.

She burst into the front room in a complete state. "Jesmonde has gone," she almost shouted. "My beloved Jesmonde has gone!"

"Who's Jesmonde?"

"It's my parrot, my beloved parrot. I was just going to introduce you but the cage door is open and so is the top part of the window. This is awful. What should I do?"

I wasn't used to situations like this but I knew the answer. "Call the police, they'll do something."

"You're right." She hurried over to the telephone. "Should I dial 999 or the local police, do you think?" She answered her own question. "It's an emergency all right but I expect the local police will be more helpful."

I was almost next to her and so I could hear what happened.

The 'phone rang and rang but at last it was answered. A bored male voice asked for Miss Feather's name and address and the purpose of the call.

"I want Jesmonde back," Miss Feather said immediately.

"Yes, madam, I expect you do but I need to know what you are talking about."

"Jesmonde is my parrot. She has gone missing. Am I talking to the right department?"

"Oh yes, madam. This is the missing parrot department all right. In fact we hardly deal with anything else."

"Then I want you to find her."

"Have you any idea where she is likely to have gone, madam?" He made the last word sound like an insult.

"Not really, but I expect she is now perching at the top of a tree."

"That's very helpful, madam, but I think we may have a bit of a problem. You see, not many of my officers have what you might call vertical take-off."

"I'm not expecting your officers to climb up trees and swing from branch to branch like Tarzan. I just want them to keep a careful watch and report any sightings."

"Well, first tell me how you spell the name of your parrot."

"J for jug, E for elephant, S for sugar, M for mince……"

"M for what, madam?"

"Mince. O for orange, N for November, D for dog, and E for elephant again."

"So that's two elephants?"

Was he trying to be funny? "That's right. Two elephants."

"Thank you, I've got a note of that. And at what time did they, sorry, I don't mean that, I mean Jesmonde, escape?"

"Any time between eight-thirty this morning and four-fifteen this afternoon."

"Thank you, that's most helpful. Now I think that's all the information we require."

"Don't you want to know her colour and what breed she is, and so on?"

"No, it's really not necessary. From our point of view, one parrot is much like another."

"I don't think you should say that. It sounds to me like pure prejudice and I'm sure you don't want another public inquiry into that."

"Look madam, I do have other things to deal with. In fact - apart from missing parrots of course - two robberies, three actual bodily harms and four burglaries. All the same, madam, you may rest assured that your missing parrot will get the amount of priority it deserves."

"Thank you, I am most grateful."

Miss Feather put the 'phone down with a groan. "Somehow, I don't think he was taking it all that seriously. But I don't see what else I can do at the moment. I'll get your juice and the Jaffa cakes straightaway."

About time too, I said to myself. But I put on my best smile. "Thank you, Miss Feather. That would be great."

But I had to wait a lot longer because almost immediately there was another loud cry from the kitchen area.

Oh Lord! I thought. What has she lost this time, her pet gorilla?

She rushed excitedly into the room.

"Miles, she's back!"

"Who's back?"

"Jesmonde. She's back. Come and see."

So I followed her along the narrow corridor into a small square room. There wasn't much in it except a computer on a table, a chair, and a large bird cage. Inside the cage a green overweight parrot was sheepishly, if that's the right word, tucking in to some bird food.

Miss Feather shut the cage door firmly. "I can hardly believe it. Where have you been, Jesmonde? I've been so worried about you, I have just called the police."

Jesmonde gave her a beady stare. "Bloody stupid," she croaked.

"I'm afraid those are the only two words she knows," Miss Feather explained apologetically.

"Have you tried teaching her to say *Pretty Polly*?" I inquired. "I thought all parrots could say that."

"Yes, I have tried that, but she just keeps on repeating her usual two words. Now, do you think I've got to 'phone the police to tell them that Jesmonde is back?"

"Yes, otherwise even without vertical take-off there could be policemen scrambling up trees all over the place."

"All right, but I'm not looking forward to it."

We made our way back to the 'phone.

To Miss Feather's obvious relief, the voice at the other end this time was female and cheerful. "Name and address, and purpose of call?"

"I reported a missing parrot a few minutes ago but I'm pleased to inform you that she has now returned."

The voice in turn sounded pleased. "That's very good news. In fact I count that as a success."

"Er...... how do you mean?"

"Well, you've just reported a missing parrot and now you tell us that it's no longer missing. I regard parrots as being in the same category as people so that means I can tick the Missing Person Recovery box. So it stands to reason we can claim the credit."

"But with respect you didn't have anything to do with her recovery."

"Miss, we do have targets to meet, you know. You don't really mind if I record this as being a successful recovery following upon a missing person report by a member of the public, do you?"

"No, all right. Chalk it up if it helps you with your target practice."

Miss Feather put the 'phone down.

She turned to me. "You know what Jesmonde would say, don't you?"

"Bloody stupid," we chorused.

Then I spent the next half-hour trying to teach Jesmonde to say *Pretty Polly*. I didn't manage it but we had a great time.

On the way home, I couldn't think about anything else. Parrots were brilliant, absolutely brilliant. I wanted one but how did you get hold of them? Could you get them on the internet? Perhaps Jesmonde would have babies and Miss Feather might give me one as a present. But that didn't seem likely. To begin with, so far as I knew, Jesmonde didn't have a husband or a partner or anything, so that could be a problem.

I thought of talking to Mum about getting a parrot, one like Jesmonde, but I knew it wouldn't be easy. The trouble is that she is always cross about something: the cost of food, the cost of heating, the weather, the noise the neighbours make at night, the state of the country, you name it. And of course she is often cross with me: my clothes, my hair, my untidy bedroom, my attitude (as she calls it) to home-work, my choice of friends, and now it would be parrots.

I suppose I could bribe her, but how? Perhaps I should have a frightful accident; then as I lay in the hospital bed I could persuade her that my only chance of recovery was to be given a parrot. But that would involve having a frightful accident which could be a bore.

So what with one thing and another, I am in a complete muddle and I can't sleep at night because of it. I still love Miss Feather, of course I do, but I think I am also in love with Jesmonde. But can I be in love with both of them? I don't know what the rules are. Somebody at school told me that it's bad for a guy to two-time a woman. I suppose that includes parrots and I don't want anybody to think that I am a two-timer.

Although she treats me like an equal, I just don't feel that I can talk to Miss Feather about any of this. So I think I'd better try to arrange to see Jesmonde again. At least I know what she will say.

DUMPED?

A two-day search of a lake for a drowned man was called off when the victim turned up looking for his clothes. The 24-year old disappeared after breaking up with his girlfriend. When his clothes were discovered by the lake, police feared the worst. When the "drowned man" appeared, he told the police that he couldn't remember why he had taken his clothes off because he had been drunk. He woke up at a nearby house where the owners had found him naked and taken him in. The man's ex-girlfriend said: "It's stupid things like this that caused me to dump him."

"Look, Andy, we've been talking on the 'phone for the last twenty minutes and getting nowhere. Why can't you just accept it that I have dumped you? It's all over, it's finished, I never want to see you again. …….. What do you mean, why? You know perfectly well why. I just can't face having to deal with all the stupid things you get up to. …….. Do you want a list? I don't know where to start. I suppose the first one was when I took all my friends to watch you hang-gliding and you forgot to get a hang-glider. …….. *You* felt stupid! Well, how do you think I felt, I've never been so embarrassed in my life and my friends all thought you were a complete twat. Then there was the occasion when we went to the fancy-dress party and you had forgotten, or said you had forgotten, that it was a fancy-dress thing and I went in that specially hired Marie Antoinette costume and you turned up in an old sweater and jeans and trainers. …….. Yes I know you claimed to be a famous pop-star but that didn't work, of course it didn't. And I may say you were already pissed out of your mind and I reckon it wasn't just booze, it was something else as well, well we won't go into details. Then there have been all those times when your stupid old car suddenly packed up, usually on the motorway, because like the prat you are you hadn't got round to putting petrol in the tank, then there's your habit of dropping things, sometimes quite valuable things such as Auntie's Ming vase, to take one example, and you may just possibly possibly possibly remember that she was very very very slightly upset, particularly as it wasn't insured. And what about the times when you insulted Granny by calling her an old tart? It just goes on and on. So that's one reason why we are finished. ……..

"What, you want me to spell out other reasons? Andy, don't push me, I might say something I regret. …….. Well, if you must know, I used to like your hair, I used to like it a lot, but frankly there's too much of it, all over the place so to speak, and you don't wash it properly: in fact the only good thing about your recent dip in the lake is that you probably emerged a good deal cleaner than when you went in. …….. No, I'm not being offensive, it's just one of the reasons why I have gone off you, you asked so I'm telling you. …….. And there's no need to shout and Oh God! Why can't you behave like a sensible human-being for a change? Anyway, as I said before, this conversation is getting us nowhere so please just accept the situation. ……..

"Look, there's no point in us meeting up again; there's nothing to discuss. I'm sorry to have to spell it out but I don't have any feelings for you now, at least I don't think I have, it's as simple as that. …….. How many more times have I got to tell you: there is no point in us seeing each other? …….. What do you mean: there's someone you would like me to meet? ……..*Who* did you say? …….. Erica. And who is she, may I inquire? ……..Eric? Don't be stupid, that's a man's name. …….. Oh yes, and who is Eric then? You've never mentioned him before. …….. Somebody you met last week? So what's so special about him? …….. My God! You're not one of those, are you? That might explain a lot. How did you meet him? …….. At one of those bars? Look, I'm very broadminded as you know, I simply don't care what goes on behind bedroom doors, but you must see that from my point of view it's a bit of a shock. I never suspected anything. …….. Oh, so you think you are AC/DC, in other words you go for both men and women. And you think that makes it all right then? Well, I'm not sure about that. Oh God! Now you are making me cry. You never said a word to me about this sort of thing and I thought we really knew each other and we didn't have any secrets. ……..

"What's the point of the three of us meeting for a drink? I don't know the guy and I'm not sure I want to. What does he look like, by the way? …….. Really? I think that makes things worse, if anything. I didn't know you would be turned on by that. …….. How can I say whether he would turn me on as I've never met him? From what you've told me, I very much doubt it, frankly. And does he happen to have a job or is he one of the great unemployed? …….. You must be joking. …….. Really? That's rather impressive, I must admit. So what else should I know about him? …….. *What*? You are planning to go away together for a long weekend? Somewhere exotic, I trust? …….. *Scunthorpe*! What on earth will you do in Scunthorpe? Oh my God! I'd better not ask. …….. You want to get to know each other better? That's nice, I hope you will be very happy. …….. No, I'm fine, I'm not really choking. …….. Yes, after all I think perhaps I ought to see him, not that it's any of my business of course. …….. Well, all right then, don't expect anything from me, that's all, and now that you have met him you probably don't need anything from me, but okay I don't mind if the three of us meet, just for a drink…… Yes, all right, usual time, usual place.

And just make sure you remember to put some clothes on this time and that you aren't pissed out of your mind when you arrive.
   " 'Bye. Love you."

THE BLACK DOG

I sat hunched up in my favourite chair. The candles were flickering and the logs in the fire were spluttering; the room was getting dark and only a little light was seeping through the small windows. From a nearby room I could hear the sound of the harpsichord being played by my beloved wife Annette who yet again was big with child. I bowed my head in silent grief at the thought of the three babies she had borne, all to die within days of their birth.

There was a knock at the door. I did not answer but a moment later the faithful William entered. He looked at me from beneath his bushy eyebrows.

"You are sad, master?" He knew me well.

"A touch of melancholy, William. It is no more than that."

"Then I will light more candles and stoke up the fire and bring you a tot of something."

"You are a good man, William. That should help me get rid of the black dog."

"The black dog, master?"

I laughed. "It is but an expression. Many great men have suffered from it and will continue to suffer from it, men such as Winston Churchill."

"Forgive me, master, but that name means nothing to me."

"Of course not, it is my fault. As I think you know, sometimes I gaze at that mirror opposite and I can see all sort of wondrous things yet to come in centuries ahead."

"Ay, master, I know of this. It is much the talk of the servants."

William busied himself in the room and departed in search of my favourite tot.

The sound of the harpsichord stopped. Annette got easily tired and would be off to lie down.

I had a short time to myself and so I rose and crossed towards the mirror. I gazed at it for full two minutes. At first I saw only my reflection and then there came the strange mistiness of the sort I had seen so many times before. The mist half-cleared and I could make out the features of a black dog.

My throat was dry and my hands were quivering.

"Is there any hope for my dear wife and myself and for our unborn child?" I whispered. "Is there any hope for the World?"

There was a long silence. The dog looked at me, completely expressionless.

Then very very slowly it began to wag its tail.

This was great news which I must impart to Annette as soon as possible! One look at my face and she would know not to inquire how I had learnt of it.

I returned to my chair. A knock at the door, and William came in bearing a tray with glasses and a small decanter on it.

He glanced at me, obviously surprised by my cheerful expression. "You are feeling better, master?"

I smiled. "Yes, much better. The black dog has gone. In fact both of them have gone."

"Both?" He was clearly startled and for a moment it seemed that he was about to drop the tray. Then his years of training took over and he advanced slowly, his hands shaking slightly, before carefully placing the tray on the table beside me.

But I could see what he was thinking. That I was mad. Barking mad.

MOBILE HOME

Nigel gazed contentedly from his balcony of the rented apartment in Palma, Mallorca, at the busy throng of people below. An excellent little holiday this was turning out to be, and today had been particularly good because he had bought a new mobile phone. This was to replace the old one - at least 12 months' old - which he had somehow dropped on to the pavement where it had shattered with an impressive scrunching noise.

The new model had a seven million pixel camera, high-speed uplink packet access to the internet, stereo Bluetooth, satnav, illuminated browser shortcut keys, six built-in games, a torch and many other facilities. You could even make and receive phone calls.

It would be fun, Nigel decided lazily, to try out his new toy by phoning his home in Battersea. Nobody would be there on a Friday afternoon but the answering service would kick in after six rings. He would leave a message to himself.

Carefully he prodded the numbers on his mobile and pushed the call button. The telephone began to ring. After four rings the phone was answered. But this was impossible! No-one apart from himself had the keys to his house except the cleaning lady who came in on Tuesday mornings.

The voice was female, educated and mildly amused.

"Hallo, Nigel's residence; can I help you?"

Nigel spluttered with astonishment. "Who are you?"

"I don't usually give my name to strangers."

"I think I must have got the wrong number. I was 'phoning my home in Battersea. I'm afraid I ...."

"No, if you are Nigel, you've got the right number. This is your home in Battersea."

"Then who on earth are you?"

"As I said, I don't usually give my name to strangers."

"But what are you doing in my house?"

There was a moment's pause. "I suppose that's a reasonable question. If you must know, I'm doing a spot of burglary."

"Is this some kind of joke?"

"That depends on your sense of humour. But I'm quite serious. Shall I tell you the items I have taken so far and lined up in the hallway?"

"How did you get in?"

"I have my methods."

"That doesn't tell me anything."

"It wasn't meant to."

"I suggest you make a run for it. I am getting my wife here to 'phone the Battersea police this very moment."

"That doesn't seem very likely. I happen to know you're not married."

"How on earth do you know that?"

"Oh, I carry out some research before I do a job. I'm no ordinary burglar, you know."

"Okay, then for your information I have two mobile phones and I am just about to 'phone my next door neighbour in Battersea. He happens to be a detective inspector."

"No, he's not, he's an estate agent and he and his family are away in Norfolk for the weekend. And if you have a second mobile phone, which I doubt, by the time you've finished talking to me - unless of course you carry on two conversations at once - and get through to the UK and manage to speak to the police and they get round here, that should give me at least ten minutes which is all I need."

"So what do you suggest I do?" Nigel heard himself inquiring rather plaintively.

The amusement in her voice came over clearly. "I'm not sure it's for me to advise you but I suppose you could just stop talking to me and then try 'phoning the police."

"I doubt if there is much point. But if you won't tell me your name, you could at least tell me something about yourself."

"Okay, I live alone with my adorable cat in a maisonette."

"Does that mean you are a cat burglar?"

"Very funny. No, it doesn't."

"Whereabouts?"

" I'm not going to say where if you don't mind, but if you really want to know about me I'm thirty-something years old and I like dining out. Also I am blonde and very tall. And without wishing to boast, I am beginning to get filthy rich."

"Filthy rich from your burglaries, I assume?"

"Oh, I'm no ordinary burglar." She sounded quite aggrieved at the idea. "I'm also a professional con-person and I'm reasonably good at computer fraud."

"Thanks for the information. But why are you telling me all this?"

Again there was a pause. The voice was now subdued. "You asked, didn't you? Anyway, I just like talking to guys sometimes. There's nothing wrong with that, is there?"

"No, no, of course not," Nigel said hastily, "but I think I should tell you I really don't go for people who are dishonest. Sorry, but that's that."

"Oh, no? You surprise me. What about those lies you told me a few seconds ago about your wife and the next door neighbour?"

Nigel was conscious that again he was on the defensive. "They just seemed to be a good idea at the time. And they weren't nearly as bad as burglary."

"That's a matter of opinion. Dishonesty is dishonesty. Anyway, I'm getting bored and I'm beginning to regret answering the phone in the first place."

"Why did you, as a matter of interest?"

"Like you said, it just seemed a good idea at the time."

There was an awkward pause. "Well, so long." Click.

On an impulse, Nigel re-dialled the number. The phone was answered after only two rings.

"Hallo, Nigel's residence; can I help you?"

"Yes, would you please not take the painting that is hanging on the wall in my bedroom? I know it's worth a lot but it's of great sentimental value to me. And would you stick your telephone number on the back of it in case I want to speak to you again? I promise I won't pass it on to the police."

There was a chuckle at the other end. "I'll think about it. But please don't 'phone again. Some people have got work to do." Click.

Nigel sat gazing thoughtfully into space. The woman's research was obviously good but how good? After fifteen minutes he put through a call to the security company he used in London, and identified himself.

"Have you anything to report? I think the painting in my bedroom may have been taken off the wall which is one of the things that should have caused the system to alert you."

The voice at the other end was positively reeking with pleasure. "Yes, sir, the system worked and we got the police round in minutes. They've just informed me that they caught the burglar red-handed. It was a woman, would you believe it, and she was just leaving your place with two large suitcases filled with your stuff. So I reckon you made a good investment when you had that system installed."

Nigel felt a tug of conflicting emotions. Good in one sense that she had been caught but on the other hand she had sounded cool and rather fun.

"Do you happen to know whether she took the painting away?"

"Now it's odd you should mention that. The constable who arrested her looked at the painting because I told him to check it. He said it was still hanging on the wall but it looked as though it had been taken off for some reason and then put back again."

Nigel smiled to himself. In a week's time he would check whether there was a phone number on the back. The trouble was that even if he found a number, it wasn't going to be of much use. Its owner would no doubt be spending a long time in Holloway and would hardly want to talk to him anyway.

"Is there anything else we can do for you, sir? We will of course be sending you a full written report."

"No, thank you; that's fine. I'm most grateful."

But actually he wasn't all that grateful. In fact, the more he thought about it, the sorrier he was that he had broken his old mobile phone. If he hadn't done that, he wouldn't have bought the new one and he wouldn't have phoned home and he wouldn't have spoken to the extraordinary woman and he wouldn't have played that trick on her about the painting and he wouldn't have found himself sitting on the balcony in an emotional heap.

The shadows were beginning to hover. He helped himself to another can of San Miguel.

Idly he switched on his phone again and began to play one of the games, Cops and Robbers. He shot three robbers within two minutes but that didn't chase away the blues; it just made him think all the more about the cool woman.

The day had turned sour. How could he get this woman out of his mind? Another swig of San Miguel. Then he moved to the edge of the balcony and, after only a moment's thought, with a quick twist of his wrist he let the phone slip away where it shattered on the pavement below.

A totally useless exercise, of course, except from the point of view of the shop-owner who sold expensive mobile phones. The following morning he could hardly believe his luck.

HORSEPLAY

Letter to The Times newspaper, 2 January 1841.
"Sir. Your reporter has overstated a case heard at the Mansion-house on Wednesday last concerning a person employed by us charged with galloping down a main street in the City. The vehicle was not a gig but a heavily covered cart and the spirited horse is a large very fat dray horse which could not gallop under any circumstances. To guard against mischief in the future, I have given strict instructions that the driver of the cart shall not proceed at a greater pace than three miles and a half within the hour. Fred Woodbridge. Red Lion Brewery."

It's a disgrace, an absolute disgrace. There am I described as "a large very fat dray horse". Okay, I am large and a touch overweight; I enjoy my oats like everyone else but how would you like to be called "very fat"? And what really gets me is that no one consulted me about any of this. Now thousands of readers are probably having a laugh at my expense.

And to add insult to injury, the letter actually states that I "could not gallop under any circumstances". Now that really is below the belt. And I can tell you - straight from the horse's mouth, as the saying goes - it's simply not true. As for proceeding at no more than "three miles and a half within the hour to guard against mischief", my master must be off his rocker. Mischief indeed! Whatever next? A man with a red flag walking ahead of every cart? The trouble is that nobody has the guts to take risks these days. We live in a mollycoddled Society, that's my view.

I suppose I ought to be pleased that I am described as being "spirited" and yes, that's true of course, but it doesn't make up for the rest of it. I wonder if the law of libel applies to dray horses? One thing my master doesn't mention is that he is a bit overweight himself: too much port if you ask me, not that I touch the stuff myself.

So what can I do about it? Well, one thought is that next week when I am out pulling that sodding cart - excuse my language but I feel strongly about all this - and we get to the hill going down from St Paul's, I will start to gallop. I am quite capable of it, really I am. I reckon that if I have one of my good days I can get up to fifteen miles per hour (none of this rubbish about "within the hour") and the driver will be hanging on for dear life. The cart might even tip over. That will teach them! Of course everyone will be angry with me but I'm not afraid of them and I'm just past caring. And my master can get knotted as far as I am concerned. With any luck he will have to go to the Mansion-house himself and take the rap if the brewery faces another charge. Not that I'm vindictive: I just like to think of people getting their come-uppance.

Now I suppose you are wondering how it is that I see The Times and how it is that I am able to read it. Well, if you must know, last week's copies are often brought to the stable and are used for mucking out and stuff, and so I get hold of them from time to time. As for reading it, that's between me and the stable-door or the gate-post if you don't mind.

But one way or another, I feel so angry about the whole thing: do you know what? I've a good mind to write to The Times.

TOP JUDGE

Sir Charles Monkford, one of Her Majesty's High Court judges, was widely regarded as a boring old fart.

Not that he was all that old, 62 to be precise, and he had certain advantages: he was tall, thin and distinguished-looking. The more catty of his critics claimed that his unexpected promotion to the High Court Bench had been entirely due to his good looks and his scholarly half-moon spectacles. The main trouble was that apart from the Law and his stamp collection he appeared to have no interests. Even his friends had to concede that his conversation tended to be on the limited side. He also had an irritating habit of saying "as it were" every few sentences. In court he was slow and pedantic. Altogether a person one would prefer not to bump into in the street or anywhere else for that matter.

But he had a vice (of a sort) which few people knew about, let alone guessed at. He had a passion for fast cars. He felt rather guilty about this which was why he drove to court each day in his elderly Volvo which obviously had seen happier days and which he parked outside his mews house at night. In the garage, safely out of sight, lurked the Porsche.

This was the car he used to drive down to the cottage in Dorset most weekends. If possible, he would get away by 3 o'clock on Friday afternoons, persuading himself that he therefore got ahead of the heavy traffic exiting from London. His wife Cynthia knew better and generally went in advance by train.

So it was that on one fine Friday afternoon in July he eased the Porsche out of the garage and onto the Cromwell Road where he joined the long slow-moving line of vehicles. Not an irritable man by temperament, he nevertheless drummed his fingers impatiently on the steering-wheel: it would be good to get shot of all this traffic so that the car could get into its stride.

Three-quarters of an hour later he was on the motorway in the outside lane bowling along at 79 miles per hour. This was his normal motorway speed because, although well over the limit, he reckoned it probably meant that if caught the chances of being prosecuted were not high. The one thing he knew was that if stopped he would be extremely polite and apologetic and would certainly not disclose his job: in the hands of a bolshie police officer any mention of his status could be disastrous. Speed cameras were of course a risk but he was pretty sure he knew where they were.

After a few minutes he glimpsed in his rear mirror a car rapidly catching up on him. It looked like a BMW coupe of some kind. He swung into the middle lane to let it pass. As it came abreast, the young loutish driver glanced towards him and made a rude gesture with two fingers. He was puzzled: so far as he knew he had done nothing to cause the driver annoyance, as it were. He slowed to a modest 77 miles per hour. Then, for reasons he was never able to explain to himself, a demon entered his soul. Why should this loutish driver get away with it? He moved over to the outside lane again and began to accelerate. He had no idea what if anything he would do if he caught up with the BMW. That remained to be decided.

His speed went up. 80..... 90...... 100......110. He hadn't driven so fast since a trip several years ago on a German autobahn. No cameras and no signs of a police car: he should be okay even though he was aware of some slightly resentful looks from more sedate drivers. In the far distance he thought he could detect the rear end of the BMW. At this rate, he chuckled to himself, he should be in Dorset in no time at all, as it were. His concentration lapsed for a moment. Then he became aware of a plethora of brake lights coming on ahead. Ye Gods! A crisis, a pile-up or something. He slammed on his brakes as hard as he could but he had underestimated his speed and his stopping distance. Even as the tyres screeched he could see that a collision was inevitable. A lorry had jackknifed across the road and a number of cars had ploughed into each other. The BMW had hit the rear of the car ahead and in turn the Porsche struck the rear of the BMW.

Mercifully no one was seriously injured and all the other cars managed to stop in time. The tail-back became enormous but the police were soon on the scene. While attempts to move the lorry and damaged cars were in progress, brief statements were taken from various drivers and passengers.

Sir Charles was extremely polite and apologetic. Then he phoned his wife on the mobile. "I'm sorry, my dear, but I have been involved in a bit of a contretemps, as it were. …… Yes, an accident on the motorway. …… No, I'm a little shaken up but I'm perfectly all right though I'm afraid the car is badly damaged. …… Yes, I will come on by train somehow. I expect I will be very late in getting to the cottage but I don't imagine there will be any repercussions, as it were."

He was right about being very late in getting to the cottage but wrong about the absence of repercussions.

Ten days later he was enjoying his breakfast muesli at the mews house when a formal-looking envelope shot through the letter-box. "Something for you, Honeybunch," Cynthia declared after a brief look at it. "I hope it isn't bad news."

The effect of the letter inside the envelope was that Sir Charles was to be prosecuted for dangerous driving and exceeding the speed limit. Not given to strong language, he contented himself with an "Oh, hell." Then he added, "I do hope there isn't going to be any adverse publicity, as it were. I can't afford that sort of thing in my job."

Cynthia had a practical side to her nature. "Get someone good to represent you and try and get off the dangerous driving charge. If you just go down on the speeding, the Press won't be much interested."

In due course the Magistrates' Court hearing took place. News that one of the defendants that morning was a High Court judge had spread but only a couple of local reporters attended with instructions to notify the Press Association if anything dramatic occurred. On the advice of his experienced solicitor, Sir Charles pleaded Not Guilty to both summonses. "No need to admit anything much," the solicitor had confided. "This Bench likes to arrive at a British compromise if it can."

The BMW driver, whose own case was to be heard later that morning, gave evidence for the Prosecution. According to him, he remembered coming up behind the Porsche which was travelling at a very moderate speed and it had kindly pulled over to the middle carriageway to let him pass. As he went by, he had given a cheerful wave of thanks and then proceeded on his way. He had later been faced with the pile-up ahead and had slammed on his brakes. He looked in his mirror and saw the Porsche which was now going too fast and was getting dangerously close; then it rammed into the back of his car.

When the time came for Sir Charles to give evidence he appeared confident and composed; no one could see the small trickle of perspiration down his back. He explained that he had been travelling at his normal speed in the outside lane, that he had pulled into the middle lane to let the BMW get by, that the driver had made an offensive gesture but that he had thought little of this and he had resumed his journey in the outside lane until confronted with the pile-up ahead.

The young prosecuting solicitor, who was wearing a crumpled pin-striped suit, shuffled among the voluminous papers on his desk and rose to cross-examine.

"I suggest that you mistook the sign the other driver gave as he passed and that you lost your temper as a result?"

"No, I very rarely lose my temper."

"I put it to you that you decided to have a race with him?"

"Certainly not. I am not a racing man."

"I hear what you say but I put it to you - and this is based on some witness statements - that not long before the collision you were driving at at least 120 miles per hour?"

"No, with respect. That is complete nonsense."

"Do you accept that you were driving in excess of 70 miles per hour?"

The unseen trickle of perspiration had become a positive flow. "I did not look at the speedometer but I recognise the possibility that I was travelling in excess of the statutory limit, as it were."

"And it was because you were travelling dangerously fast that you failed to stop in time and collided with the vehicle ahead?"

"I do not accept that. I was suddenly faced with a serious emergency and I did all I could to avoid a collision."

The solicitor gave a faint bleat, looked down at his notes, decided he had done enough and sat down.

Twenty minutes later, after a persuasive speech on behalf of Sir Charles to the magistrates, the latter acquitted in respect of the dangerous driving but found the speeding allegation proved. Sir Charles was fined and had his licence endorsed.

As Cynthia had rightly predicted, the National Press showed little interest but a couple of newspapers carried a brief column under the heading *Speedy Top Judge*.

Over a cup of coffee at the Royal Courts of Justice, two of Sir Charles's colleagues sat spluttering with mirth as they read these columns.

"A pity there's no mention of what speed he was actually doing," one of them observed. "Apparently there was a suggestion that he was doing well over the ton."

The other one laughed. "You must be joking. I can't imagine dear Charles winding that old Volvo up to more than 50 mph even downhill and with a following wind. Boring old fart."

BEWITCHED

I sat watching the man slurping back his beer. Middle-aged, small drooping moustache, reddish nose, watery eyes, brown suit, grubby open-necked shirt. Yuck!

He must have been aware of my gaze. He shifted and half turned towards me before eyeing me up and down.

"Are you a witch?" he inquired after a short pause.

"I beg your pardon?"

"I said, *Are you a witch?*"

"Do me a favour! Why do you ask that?"

He leered at me, revealing a row of nasty teeth. "It's the way you are dressed. A big funny hat and a long sort of cloak."

"Thanks a lot. That's the way I like to dress. If you don't mind."

He muttered something to himself and took another swig of beer. He looked at me again, this time with an odd expression. "No offence (he slurred the word), I'm sure. You just look a bit batty to me. Your glass is empty. Want another drink?"

Good God! Surely the man didn't have designs on me. "No thank you."

"Where do you come from?"

"Near here."
"House or flat?"
"Just a place."
"Yeah, but I asked you: house or flat?"
"As I said, just a place."
"You don't give much away about yourself, do you?"
"No, I don't. Is that a problem?" Couldn't he see that I just wanted to be left in peace?
"I still think there's something weird about you."
"Like what?"
He studied me critically, or at least as critically as his half-drunken state allowed. "It's your face more than anything."
"What about my face?"
"Well, for a start you could be almost any age, you have strange dark eyes, a big nose and altogether you look, no offence meant as I said before, well...... craggy."
"What do you mean, *craggy*? Attractively rugged, perhaps?" I reckoned that would get a reaction from him.
"No, I bleeding well don't mean that. I mean, full of crags. Ugly."
That was enough. More than enough. I stood up and grabbed him by the neck. He was so shocked he didn't have time to speak. Then I hit him over the head with my glass. Hard. He rolled off his chair and slumped to the ground.
I picked up my broomstick and sailed off. I could see he was still conscious; there was a look of disbelief in his eyes as he watched me fly away.
I heard afterwards that he tried to give a description of me to the police. But of course they didn't believe him. "Who does he think he's kidding?" the sergeant asked his mates. They shook their heads in suitable bewilderment. "I suppose he expects us to find any old woman with a broomstick and then put her up on an ID parade."
Just at that moment the cleaning lady came into their office carrying a broom.
"You'll do," they cried, falling about.

She didn't see what was so funny. She told me that the same evening.

In our coven.

DUCKING THE QUESTION

"Disgusting, that's what I call it," Edwina announced to her daughter as a bunch of male genitalia came into view dangerously close to her deck-chair. "Don't look, Chloe."

The July sun blazed down on the beach and a small group of young men had dispensed with their skimpy swimming gear before chasing each other towards the sea.

Chloe, aged eleven, put aside her book and made a careful study of the offending objects from behind her rectangular sunglasses. "I don't think they are disgusting," she said after a pause. "They just look silly to me. What do you think, Tom?"

Her brother, three years older, was morosely hurling pebbles into the sea. He went pink in the face. At the moment, sex was an embarrassment to him, as Chloe well knew. Two days ago, he had forgotten to lock the bathroom door and she had charged in and caught him standing in the bath doing something rather extraordinary over a rubber duck. She had never seen anything like this before but, instinctively, had understood the situation. "That's gross!" she had exclaimed. "And it's very unfair to our duck." The incident had not been mentioned since, but Tom knew it was just a matter of time.

And here it was. "By the way, what were you doing the other day with that rubber duck?"

Tom blushed to the depth of his hormonal roots. "Nothing," he muttered, clambering to his feet. "I am going for a walk." He set off almost at a run.

Edwina looked at the departing figure. "What were you saying about a duck?"

Chloe decided to beat a partial retreat. "Nothing really. I just went into the bathroom the other day and saw him trying to drown our duck."

"How extraordinary! But at your age you've no business to go into the bathroom when he is there. You never know what you might see."

"That's true," Chloe agreed. Yes, it had been a bit strange, but - returning to the tribulations of the heroine in her romantic novel - not half as much fun as being chased by a rampant werewolf.

"Chloe," her mother interrupted a few minutes later. "Those men are coming back. Disgusting, I call it."

But this time Chloe didn't look up. Instead she decided to ask Tom what he thought it would be like to be chased by a rampant werewolf. It would make him blush again and with luck it might even bring out more spots on his face. Excellent!

Her mother glanced at her. No, she wouldn't say anything else about those men. At least her daughter had a nice book to read. She felt a twinge of envy. Such an adorable little person!

Chloe's concentration lapsed for a few seconds. What would Tom say about the werewolf? Oh, of course, he would duck the question, unlike the heroine in her novel who was fiercely resisting the efforts of the creature. She sighed happily. Life was wicked!

About ten minutes later, Tom cautiously sauntered back, sat down, and started throwing pebbles into the sea again.

Chloe registered his presence almost immediately. "Tom, I've got a question to ask you." The way she spoke gave the game away.

Tom was already on his feet and running along the beach.

Edwina looked puzzled. "How odd! What were you going to ask him?"

Another half-truth was called for. "Well, you see, Miranda - she's the amazing person in my book - is having a spot of bother so I was going to ask Tom what he thought she should do about it."

Edwina laughed affectionately. "You're so sweet, the way you try to get your brother involved. But he just seems to want to do his own thing these days. He's becoming quite a young man, isn't he?"

"Yes," Chloe said. "Actually, I've noticed that. Why do you think, though, that he keeps on ducking questions?"

"I can't imagine."

Chloe returned to her novel. Disappointingly, the werewolf was in full retreat. She'd better think up a new question for Tom. And she would wring an answer out of him if it was the last thing she ever did. After all, her questions were simple enough. Oops! The heroine's virtue was at risk again, but this time the threat came from Spacemen arriving on parachutes.

Tom reached the end of the beach and waded into the sea towards some deserted rocks. He clambered up and lay sprawled out, pondering how he might get his own back on Chloe for the trouble she was always causing him. Then a sudden thought struck him and he sat up. He remembered an old film he had watched on TV. There was a scene in which Amazon tribesmen had circled round an unfortunate young woman who was about to be made a human sacrifice. With a small stretch of the imagination, the young woman could easily be his annoying sister. No reason why he couldn't become one of the tribesmen. The thought cheered him up no end. Within moments he was mentally whooping and prancing with his fellow tribesmen around the circle. Not real revenge of course but satisfying all the same.

When later he strolled back along the beach, Chloe looked up. Oh good! Now she could ask him another of her questions. Then she saw, surprise, surprise! that he was looking positively cheerful *and* he was actually grinning at her. Okay, another time, she said to herself after a moment's thought. Although she didn't realise it, she had just learnt one of Life's important lessons: occasionally it's best to keep quiet.

Back to the book. The Spacemen were making fantastic progress!

Tom flung himself down on his nearby towel. Contentedly he began to hurl pebbles into the sea. It was a struggle not to laugh out loud. Oh dear, oh dear! The tribesmen were doing some really horrible things to his sister. Should he perhaps try to save her? No, absolutely not, or to use a phrase he had picked up at school recently, Not on your Nelly.

Over the top of her magazine, Edwina studied her offspring with maternal pride. How lucky she was to have two such marvellous children! As she shifted happily in her deck-chair she gave a nostalgic sigh. If only she herself could recapture the innocence of youth! The sheer innocence.

BABY TALK

There's something you ought to know about me straightaway. I am only ten months old but my mental age is somewhere about ten. Ten years, I mean. I don't know how it happened; I suppose I am a sort of freak. But I look like any other baby (boy or girl, and I'm not going to tell you which) and although Mummy and Daddy realise there's something strange about me they haven't really cottoned on. That may be because I decided to keep pretty quiet about it. Well, you wouldn't want everybody to know that you're a freak, would you?

Actually the whole thing has become a bit of a bore. Have you ever thought how tedious life is as a baby? Of course it has its compensations: on the whole you are kept clean and fed regularly and you can dose off much of the time. And when you want to attract attention it's dead simple: you just start crying or burping or something and within seconds you are picked up and given the whole cooee adult treatment. And it's quite fun to hurl one's rattle out of the pushchair over and over again. But the downside is that you're utterly dependent on adults: they tickle your chin and make stupid gurgling noises and talk about you as though you weren't there, and there's only so much you can do to keep them in check. You aren't given any choice about anything, that's what really gets me. I'm put in the cot when I don't want to be and then expected to go straight off to sleep; if I am asleep I'm woken up when I don't want to be; then I'm given strange mushy food; sometimes I am put in the pushchair and wheeled along the smelly and noisy streets even when it's raining. "Our baby must get as much fresh air as possible," they say; fresh air my foot, who do they think they're kidding?

And life is a bit frightening at times. The other day I was being wheeled through a Supermarket and I saw a sign which said *Baby Change*. Did it mean that if Mummy or Daddy got fed up with me, they could just swap me for another baby? Most unfair I would call that; not that anyone would ask my views about it of course. Though come to think of it, as they don't know my little secret you could hardly expect them to consult me about that or anything else. So I just snivelled a bit and threw my rattle out of the pushchair. Well, you would have done the same, wouldn't you?

I suppose that what bugs me the most is the way grown-up people who ought to know better try to attract a baby's attention. Women are the worst; most men are just politely bored. Perhaps it's something to do with the maternal instinct or perhaps it's a way of drawing attention to themselves but women don't seem to be able to stop smiling at babies and picking them up and saying silly things. Like, "Oh isn't he/she beautiful? *Such* a lovely baby! Takes after his/her Mum I can see. Fantastic eyes! Amazing! And such a sunny little personality. Really great! You must be very proud." And so on and so on. It makes me puke, literally sometimes. Just as well they can't hear what I am saying about them under my breath. It tends to be on the lines, *Stupid cow, what do you mean, sunny personality indeed, take your filthy hands off me and stop talking complete* er…. *rubbish*.

Now I imagine you're thinking I am a selfish little brat and as a matter of fact I would agree with you. Aren't most babies? The difference is that I know that I am and the rest don't: in fact they haven't got a clue, poor little perishers. They simply bumble along from day to day without a care in the world about anything or anyone except themselves. The trouble begins when they become older and bigger and throw tantrums instead of rattles. Then grown-ups start to get cross with them: "Stop being so selfish," they say. But I can't help thinking that it's the grown-ups who are selfish in the first place for having the babies.

Okay, so now you think I am being cynical, and again I would probably agree with you. But look at the time! I am going for a bit of shut-eye if you don't mind or even if you do. Nice talking to you. Aren't I fantastic and totally amazing? Just don't say *Such a lovely baby*, that's all I ask.

BIG EARS

A burglar with distinctive large ears has been warned to give up crime. He was jailed for robbery last week after witnesses described a gang that held up a bank near Preston, Lancashire. A detective said, "This man only needs to look at himself in the mirror to realise crime is not for him. He must be a total liability when he is part of a gang – he stands out a mile."

The four middle-aged men who met together in a gloomy basement flat to plan their next robbery would not have had much chance of winning prizes in a beauty contest. Although their leader "Foxy" was tall, thin, and only slightly balding, his appearance was marred by pock-marks; the others were "The Weasel" (because of his face), "Lofty" (because of his diminutive size) and "Big Ears" (for obvious reasons).

Foxy studied the members of his gang with a mixture of amusement and something close to affection. The Weasel was bright enough, unlike the other two, but they all had their own strengths, and together in the past they had pulled off five armed robberies which had gone without a hitch. The time had come for the sixth.

He cleared his throat importantly. "Our next job will be this coming Friday. The bank we are going to target has its biggest delivery of weekly cash between eleven and eleven-thirty every Friday. Now here's the plan." He spoke slowly and clearly for nearly ten minutes.

The Weasel listened attentively. Lofty and Big Ears, who both had short attention spans, found their minds wandering but they got the gist: when the security man emerged from his vehicle, Foxy would leap from the waiting Audi and threaten him with a loaded shot-gun, the Weasel would physically separate the man from the case he would be carrying, if necessary with the aid of improvised cutters, Big Ears would stand nearby with another shot-gun to threaten any passers-by who tried to intervene, and Lofty would remain in the driver's seat to make the get-away. All the men would wear stocking masks. Another car would be parked at a safe distance where they would abandon the Audi (hired by Foxy using a false driving-licence). They would be dropped off separately and would meet up two days later in the basement flat where Foxy would distribute the money in equal shares. This should be not less than £75,000 each and probably more.

"Any questions?"

"Yeah. What about them cameras, CVTV or whatever?" The Weasel's nervous tic was playing up.

Foxy looked almost hurt. "Just trust me. Why do you think I've been sussing the joint for the last couple of weeks? You don't need to worry about CCTV's. There's only one camera over the front entrance and it doesn't cover the area where we will be operating. Any more questions?"

"What do we know about the case with the cash inside? Is it one of them that will blow up in your face, like, or spray the goods with something nasty?"

"I know what you mean, diabolical things. There should be a law against them, that's my view. But no, this type of case won't cause us trouble. Anyway, I know how to open them without much hassle. So are we all set?"

There was a murmur of assent. The plan was on.

It was a bright sunny morning, that Friday. At a few minutes past eleven, Juliet was chatting on her mobile phone as she walked briskly along the pavement in the direction of the bank. Suddenly she became aware of an uproar. A man was getting out of a security van carrying a case, a car screeched up to it, three men wearing stocking masks spilled out, two of them were holding guns and the security man was pushed to the ground. Instinctively Juliet switched on the mobile phone camera and touched the button. As she did so, the man nearest to her swung round, his gun pointing straight at her. "Get back, you bitch," he shouted. "One more step and I'll shoot."

It was all over within seconds. The case was somehow torn from the security man who lay sprawled on the ground and the men leapt into the car which raced away.

The usual throng of people gathered immediately; the security man was helped to his feet; the police arrived within minutes; statements were taken. Juliet mentioned the photograph she had managed to obtain. It was whisked away for enlargement.

By two o'clock the same day a detective inspector and his young sergeant were studying it closely. The picture showed the blurred face of a man wearing a mask. But one thing, or more accurately, two things stuck out. The man's ears were clearly enormous.

The sergeant gave a shout of triumph. "That's Big Ears, sir. I came across him on the Bolton job three or four years ago: there's no mistaking him and what's more I'm pretty sure where we can lay our hands on him."

So later that very same day Big Ears found himself in the interview room at the police station. He was in a state of shock which was perhaps why he had declined to have a solicitor present. Anyway, he knew from past experience that the best thing to do was to reply "No comment" to every question put to him.

After a frustrating ten minutes, the detective inspector gave a brief nod to the sergeant sitting next to him and the latter discreetly switched off the recording machine.

Big Ears watched this, shivering inwardly. "Oh yeah? So I suppose you are going to beat me into a load of bleeding pulp now, are you?" he asked.

The inspector looked scandalised. "Certainly not! We stopped doing that sort of thing years ago." He gave a nostalgic sigh. "It's too risky these days. We play things by the book now, well most of the time. All I want to do is to have a little confidential chat, don't you think that's a good idea?"

Big Ears remained silent.

"You see, Sonny Boy, we've got you: I've shown you the photo and you know and I know and any god-damned jury will know that it's you. And you've got form. So the judge will be thinking in terms of Public Protection with the result that I reckon you are looking at fourteen years minimum. So I suggest you help us and we will help you."

"Help you? What do you mean, help you?"

"I will give it to you straight. You tell us who was in the gang and we'll make sure the judge knows about the help you've given us - particularly if we recover the cash - and you will be sent down for half or less of what you would otherwise get."

"I'm not grassing."

"Don't look at it like that. If you aren't willing to spill the beans on everybody, okay I will go along with that. Just tell me who ran the show and where the cash is likely to be."

"I'm not grassing."

"How much do you reckon was in the case?"

"That tape is still off? About three hundred grand."

"You are well-informed but I can tell you it was three hundred and eighty grand. Now what do you think is going to happen to all that nice lolly? You aren't going to get any of it for sure so what do you think your boss will do with your share? Keep it for himself of course: he's not going to share that out with the others, is he?"

Big Ears thought about Foxy for a few moments; no, he wasn't called Foxy for nothing; he couldn't be trusted, not really.

The inspector watched carefully and moved in for the kill. "Why should he have his ninety-five grand plus your ninety-five grand, all tax-free of course, while you just rot away behind bars for the next fourteen years? Okay, if you don't want to tell me out aloud, here's what we can do. I'll give you a bit of paper and a pen. Just write down his name and where we can find him and leave us to do the rest."

So Big Ears grassed.

Foxy was arrested early the following morning. The presence of shot-guns, ammunition, masks, a rough sketch of the bank, plus the opened security case stacked with money, all found in his bedroom cupboard, clearly meant that the Defence was likely to have an uphill task.

Some months later the police officers were enjoying a celebratory drink. The detective inspector was in an exceptionally mellow mood. "A good result all round, lads, don't you think? But we musn't forget my bright young sergeant here: after all, you're the guy who identified Big Ears in the first place."

"Don't mention it, sir. He stood out a mile. But I still think we ought to have told the judge about the help he gave."

ROUND ROBIN

Hallo again! Yes, it's that time of year for your annual report from George and Anthea, and what a fantastic year it has been!

The biggest excitement came in February when the roof of our house blew off! Apparently there was some sort of tornado and one moment we were watching Hercule Poirot (a repeat of course!) on the tele and the next moment we were roofless! We dialled 999 but the various services were not as helpful as we had hoped; indeed the ambulance service were quite rude. They seemed to blame us because nobody had been injured! It's enough to make one vote for the Lib Dems. And our insurance company took weeks to sort the whole thing out so what with one thing and another we had to rely on a piece of tarpaulin until Easter. It was most unsightly and matters weren't helped by a batty old woman who knocked on the door to inquire whether we knew that we had a tile missing!

In March, it was of course Anthea's birthday - no, don't ask! - and to celebrate we went to hear a concert of Beethoven's Sonatas given by a Russian pianist. We can't pronounce his name, let alone spell it! He used to be very distinguished but it soon became apparent that he was well over the top. Poor man, he clearly couldn't remember much of the music and often had to improvise with the result that part of the Sonata in E flat sounded very much like *Walking My Baby Back Home.* We suppose that at the age of ninety-three some imperfections must be expected.

By Easter we felt the need to escape and, emboldened by our successful holiday in northern France two years ago, we decided to fly to Tenerife! Our hols got off to a worrying start because we went to the wrong airport! Stansted and Luton are of course easily confused. We were in luck, however, because as soon as we discovered our mistake we rushed off to the other airport, thinking that we were bound to miss our 'plane, only to be greeted by the good news that there was a 5 hour delay. The flight was rather bumpy and most of the passengers sitting near us threw up. Also, there was a mishap when we were about to land as the pilot forgot to lower the undercarriage; fortunately he remembered in the nick of time. Otherwise it was absolutely fine. We arrived at our apartment well after midnight because of the delay, just in time to hear the rock band from the night club immediately beneath us get under way! We didn't get much sleep that night or, come to think of it, any night but it was good to think of other people enjoying themselves.

Tenerife is a beautiful island, rather like the Isle of Wight but with slightly better weather. One of the great things about it is that most of the tourists are Brits so one doesn't have to mix. Another advantage which we realised after a couple of days is that many of the natives speak English so, as it turned out, there was no need to shout. Altogether, strongly recommended and we hope to return. So if any of you good folk are like-minded, just tell us when and where: we might be able to make up one happy party!

You will want to know how the children - now both in their late-twenties, we can hardly believe it! - are getting on. Well, David's business is obviously booming because he wrote a few weeks ago to tell us that he has acquired a partner! He enclosed a photograph of them both celebrating something or other and certainly Dominic is a good-looking young man. David says that he is a railway porter but we think that must be David's little joke because of course David is a loss-adjuster and the two jobs would hardly tie in with one another. We shall see. The other exciting news is that Melanie who still works near Kings Cross in the service industry is expecting a baby! For some reason she doesn't seem keen to tell us who the lucky father is and we don't really see wedding bells ringing in the immediate future, but we are both thrilled to think that we will soon be grand-parents! At the moment we are hoping for a boy or a girl.

We also have great news about the other young people in our lives! Stephen and Flo both did brilliantly in their last term at school. We won't bore you with their exam results but we can send you full details if you like. Stephen is nearly eighteen and has a girl-friend already! Apparently she comes from Latvia but is said to be quite nice. He is about to take a gap year, working on a farm in Wales, before reading media studies at some university in the Midlands. He is not sure yet what he wants to do in the future but thinks he might become a newscaster. Time will tell. Flo is intending to become a plumber because she says that's where the money is these days. As we told Maurice and Isabel we really can't approve of this in view of her extremely successful career at school and we think she should join one of the old professions but, as we also told them, we can't possibly interfere. Hen (that's Henrietta of course) is less gifted academically than the others but, as you know, she has enormous guts and, despite her unusual height and build, came fifth in a recent charity-run! She should go far. Incidentally the charity-run raised over forty pounds! Luke did well in rehab and has more or less given up glue-sniffing. He has become interested in oceanography and so is learning to swim. We only wish he would manage to overcome his exhibitionist streak: it's a pity that the family lives so close to Hampstead Heath. Again, we are the last people to interfere but in view of our experience with David's problem when he was sixteen we were able to give helpful advice as to how to deal with the matter; we fear this was not as well received as it should have been!

Sadly in May, Beatrice, our faithful old Mini, finally came to rest (in the middle of the Blackwall tunnel; the tail-back was sensational!) so we decided we had to buy a new car. Our test-run in a little Japanese model went well until George reversed into a stupidly-placed brick wall. After that we weren't very keen to buy the car but the salesman, who had previously seemed nice, unexpectedly became most offensive. In the end, as it no longer had any rear wings, he let us have it for a reduced price, so we count that as a success. Welcome Beatrice the Second!

The following month, Bob our next door neighbour was awarded an MBE for services to Waste Disposal! In view of Julia's psychotic episodes and her worrying attitude towards the Royals, he kindly invited us to go to the investiture instead. We felt really grand entering the portals of Buckingham Palace! Before the ceremony began, an official wearing a tail coat told everyone in the audience to remain silent and not to give the Recipients the clap which they deserved. Everything was fine until the moment when Bob's name was called. Then he went forward and had the misfortune to trip and fall flat on his face almost beneath Her Majesty. The whole Stateroom went quiet and the conductor of the orchestra dropped his baton. The Queen looked for a moment as though she was amused but it may just have been a trick of the light because she was very gracious about it and told Bob not to worry as that sort of thing happened every other year or so. Our hopes of having a few words with Her Majesty were dashed as she scarpered pretty quickly; in fairness she probably had other things to do. So we took Bob to a gastro-pub for a congratulatory lunch of sausages and mash followed by figs; we felt he was in need of it!

July saw us giving our usual garden party; we mustn't boast but we think the event has become almost legendary even though our garden may be on the small side. We won't regale you with a list of all the distinguished people who came although we were particularly fortunate to have one of our local councillors! We do wish you could see the many thank-you letters we received (which of course we have kept), every single one of them, after mentioning the torrential rain, paying tribute to our fantastic hospitality!

In August we abandoned plans to go to our favourite haunt in Skegness and instead stayed at home to look after Molly our tabby cat who was very poorly. With the aid of the vet - we won't tell you what the fees were! - and, needless to say, a great deal of loving care on the part of yours truly, she is now much better and is back on four feet, most of the time.

In September we caught a glimpse of two birds in our garden which we think may have been blue-tits. We hope they will come back next year.

At the beginning of October we decided - yet again! - that we should make a real effort to get fit by taking up an active recreation. We ruled out archery because of that unfortunate incident last year, though mercifully George has almost completely recovered from the wound. The badminton hall is closed because of rising damp and so we decided to join a dancing class. As many of you will remember, Anthea won a school prize at the age of fifteen - yes, we know it's some time ago! - for her cha-cha-cha but as she had only danced two or three times in the last thirty years she understandably felt a bit rusty. George had never danced a single step but he became a real expert by watching *Strictly Come Dancing* and liked to think of himself as one of the judges! We were a bit thrown at first to discover that all our fellow students - most of them wore jeans! - were less than half our age but on the whole they were quite supportive and, after only three lessons, someone kindly described our Tango as spectacular! We intend to give a costumed demonstration of it at our forthcoming Christmas party at home despite the fact that floor space is of course rather limited. It should be a memorable event!

So yet another great year draws to a close and we are looking forward to writing next year's newsletter already! Don't forget to send us a short letter with all your news if you have any; we will certainly read it if we can find the time. In the meanwhile, Season's Greetings!

ARE YOU COURTING?
(Extracts from the author's one-act play)

Monday morning in Sebastian's room.

Sebastian (*a barrister*) I'm going over to court now to chat up my solicitor before my case starts. So, Kate, why don't you watch a Master's summons first? Cuthbert has got one. You can come along to the Chancery Division afterwards. Assuming you can find it.

Kate (*his pupil*) That's OK with me, but I don't think I know Cuthbert.

Sebastian I'll introduce you. He's a University don so of course he doesn't like coming face to face with students. But he should be OK with you. He practises part-time as a barrister. Says he prefers the smell of the arena to the dust of the senior common-room. And talking of smells, he specialises in sewage and drains. There is a lot in drains, you know.

Kate Is he the person who wrote the main textbook on the subject?

Sebastian Yes, it's called *The Effluent Society*. It would be a best-seller if only he brought the price down by about two hundred pounds. Let's go.

In Lucy's office.

Mr Diabolical (*a frequent client*) enters.

Lucy (*a solicitor, half-rising and waving him to a chair*) How good to see you again! Do sit down. (*She opens and struggles with a bulging file*) Which case are we dealing with now? Or is this something new?

Mr Diabolical It's diabolical. Absolutely diabolical. (*He starts to remove lower items of his clothing*)

Lucy What are you doing?

Mr Diabolical You'd better look at my foot. It's a mess.

Lucy But I am a solicitor, not a chiropodist.

Mr Diabolical I know you are but I want you to see the evidence while it is fresh.

Lucy I'm not sure that "fresh" is the word I would have used (*as he extends a foot towards her*) but yes, I can see you've got a red scratch mark.

Mr Diabolical That's what she did. That's where the buggy ran into me. Diabolical it was. I want to sue her.

Lucy Let's get some details first. And would you mind putting your sock and shoe back on, please? Who was it?

Mr Diabolical It was Miss Casanova of course. You know, the single mother living next door to me. Always causing trouble, that tart.

Lucy Tell me what happened.

Mr Diabolical There I was, minding my own business as usual. Just about to go indoors when this woman came along, bold as brass, pushing a buggy. And do you know what? There was a baby inside.

Lucy Was that a surprise?

Mr Diabolical Yes, it was a brand new one.

Lucy Buggy or baby?

Mr Diabolical Baby. Ugly little brat it was. That woman has got two of them already except that they're getting older. As you know, I am the last person to cause trouble but if there is one thing I can't stand it's having screaming kids next door.

Lucy Did you say anything to her?

Mr Diabolical No, nothing, not a word. Not a word. (*He pauses and looks away*) Well, maybe a word or two, maybe. Come to think of it, I did. All I said was: "How many more little bastards are you going to produce?"

Lucy Do go on.

Mr Diabolical This woman started screeching like a diabolical scalded parrot and suddenly took a run at me with her buggy. I was so shocked I didn't even have time to jump out of the way. Straight into me she went. It's a very nasty injury, as you can see.

Lucy What did you do?

Mr Diabolical I lifted up the buggy and threw it over the wall.

Lucy Good Grief! Was the baby still inside?

Mr Diabolical No, the baby shot out when the buggy hit me. I never did find out what happened to it.

Lucy Was the buggy damaged?

Mr Diabolical Not much. Hardly at all, really. One of the wheels came off. That's all, (*pause*) well, possibly both wheels, (*pause*) and the hood.

Lucy Whether or not you've got a claim against her, she may have a claim against you. Do you really want to go on with this?

Mr Diabolical I certainly do. Look what she's done to my foot.

Lucy Thank you, I've seen more than enough. Why don't you hurry off now to the A & E department of your local hospital and then just follow the signs marked "Adult Buggy-Injuries"?

Later the same morning. Sebastian's room.

Sebastian and Kate enter and go to their desks. Sebastian opens the brief for the afternoon's case.

Sebastian How did Cuthbert get on with his summons before the Master?

Kate Cuthbert wouldn't take No for an answer. He kept on trying to persuade the Master to alter a previous order. After ten minutes, the Master exploded and said, "I am *functus*."

Sebastian What did Cuthbert say?

Kate He said, "I'm sorry to hear that, Master. You look well enough to me." So he lost, and we all left. But Cuthbert is very clever. He can bow as he walks backwards. Anyway, I got to your court in time. It was packed.

Sebastian What did you make of it all?

Kate Cool, really cool. Just like a French farce, but much funnier. The barristers kept bobbing up and down and asking the judge to make "the usual order". Then your case was called on and you asked the judge to stand it over for twenty-eight days. All the judge said was, "So be it."

Sebastian Yes, it's an important function of the judiciary to say "So be it". Sounds much more impressive than "Very well". The case was adjourned because my solicitor said both sides wanted time to settle. Panic over!

Kate The solicitor liked you. He said as we were leaving, "Thank you for your help."

Sebastian Oh God, yes! That's a bad sign. It's the last I'll see of him. It's like a judge saying that a barrister has said and done everything possible for their client. It sounds good but it means that the judge wasn't impressed.

Kate As we were coming out of court, a little old barrister struggled to his feet and said, "My Lord, I am ineffective." Is he really all that ineffective?

Sebastian Far from it! He's probably the best lawyer at the Chancery Bar. He can spot a Breach of Trust even before there is one.

Lucy's office. About four-thirty.

Lucy is working at her desk. Jenny (a trainee solicitor) enters.

Jenny What happened in your court case?

Lucy I had to wait before we got on. The judge was giving judgment against a litigant in person who then said he wanted to appeal. The judge said, "You need leave to appeal," and the litigant said, "Of course I'm going to leave to appeal. I'm not going to hang around here no longer." "No, no," the judge explained, "I mean that you need my leave, my permission, to appeal." "*Your* permission to appeal," the man said, "You must be joking. As you're the person I'm complaining about, I would have thought you were the last person to decide whether I can appeal."

Jenny Oh Lord! How did the judge deal with that?

Lucy He seemed a bit thrown, but he just bowed his head in silent prayer and then after a few seconds he got his act together and explained about applying to the Court of Appeal. When he asked the man whether he wanted a stay of execution, the man went as white as a sheet and said, "But I thought hanging was abolished years ago."

Sebastian's room. About the same time.

Sebastian and Kate enter and go to their desks.

Sebastian So, Kate, would you call that an instructive day so far?

Kate Yes, it was cool the way your case was slotted in at the Crown Court this morning.

Sebastian That was thanks to Rambo.

Kate Rambo?

Sebastian It's the nickname the court staff have for the little usher with the thick glasses, the wheeze, and the hacking cough.

Kate He seemed to have some hold over the judge, though.

Sebastian Oh yes, judges have to do what their ushers tell them. Otherwise, their lives are made a complete misery.

Kate I watched a bit of the trial ahead of us. The judge asked how many more witnesses there were and counsel said he only had two more *live* witnesses. The jury looked shocked. They obviously thought the rest must be dead. Then when you got on, the judge just said "I need not trouble you".

Sebastian That's judge-speak for, "Don't say a word or you'll screw the whole thing up". And what did you think of our personal injury case this afternoon?

Kate Great! You tied the Defendant up into knots when you were cross-examining him.

Sebastian That sounds a bit kinky! But it probably helped because it made my opponent whisper, "Let's talk outside," which is barristers' code for, "Oh shit, I've got to make you an offer". So I asked the judge to adjourn for five minutes.

Kate Why was he so sceptical about the five minutes?

Sebastian Because barristers usually say "five" when they mean "fifteen". But we managed it. Though his clerk almost ruined the whole thing by coming out after four minutes and barking, "Are you ready yet?"

Kate I thought he looked and behaved rather like the judge himself.

Sebastian Yes, after a time, judges' clerks tend to resemble their owners.

Kate But you settled for seventy-eight thousand pounds?

Sebastian I tried to squeeze more out of my opponent but the claims manager - the one with the ulcer - dug his heels in.

Kate It was odd when we went back into court and you told the judge the amount. He looked as though he'd expected an entirely different sum.

Sebastian Yes, but he quickly recovered and gave a quick nod of approval. That's another important judicial function, though it's less enthusiastic than "So be it".

Kate Then everyone bowed and said how obliged they were to everyone else. Did anyone mean it?

Sebastian Good Lord, no! It's just a quaint old tradition.

Kate But it made a great end to the whole show. Now, what entertainment do we have tomorrow?

Sebastian Really Kate! You shouldn't call it *entertainment*. This is a serious profession.

Kate You could have fooled me.

Printed in Great Britain by
Amazon.co.uk, Ltd.,
Marston Gate.